Welcome to the October Harlequin Presents!

This month read Sandra Marton's *The Sheikh's Defiant Bride*, the first book in her exciting trilogy THE SHEIKH TYCOONS. We also visit the Mediterranean, and two affluent heroes who aren't afraid to take what they want, in Julia James's *Greek Tycoon, Waitress Wife* and Robyn Donald's *His Majesty's Mistress*. Things begin to heat up at work (or should we say *after* work) for Abby in Anne Oliver's *Business in the Bedroom*. Maggie Cox also brings you a sexy office tale, this time involving an Italian tycoon and his unsuspecting personal assistant, in *Secretary Mistress, Convenient Wife*. Helen Bianchin weaves a story of attraction and convenience in *Purchased: His Perfect Wife*, in which cash-strapped Lara finds herself making a deal with her brooding stepbrother. Innocence is lost and passion abounds in *One Night with His Virgin Mistress* by Sara Craven, and housekeeper Liv's job description is more hands-on than most in *Housekeeper at His Beck and Call*, compliments of Susan Stephens.

We'd love to hear what you think about Harlequin Presents. E-mail us at Presents@hmb.co.uk, or join in the discussions at www.iheartpresents.com and www.sensationalromance.blogspot.com, where you'll also find more information about books and authors!

Even if at times work is rather boring,
there is one person making the office a whole
lot more interesting: the boss!

Dark and dangerous, alpha and powerful,
rich and ruthless… He's in control, he knows
what he wants and he's going to get it!
He's tall, handsome and breathtakingly attractive.
And there's one outcome that's never in doubt—
the heroines of these supersexy
stories will be

Undressed
BY THE BOSS

From sensible suits...into satin sheets!

A brand-new miniseries available only from
Harlequin Presents!

Anne Oliver

BUSINESS IN
THE BEDROOM

Undressed
BY THE BOSS

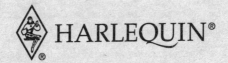

HARLEQUIN®

TORONTO • NEW YORK • LONDON
AMSTERDAM • PARIS • SYDNEY • HAMBURG
STOCKHOLM • ATHENS • TOKYO • MILAN • MADRID
PRAGUE • WARSAW • BUDAPEST • AUCKLAND

ISBN-13: 978-0-373-12770-2
ISBN-10:   0-373-12770-7

BUSINESS IN THE BEDROOM

First North American Publication 2008.

Copyright © 2008 by Anne Oliver.

All about the author...
Anne Oliver

When not teaching or writing, **ANNE OLIVER**
loves nothing more than escaping into
a book. She keeps a box of tissues handy—
her favorite stories are intense, passionate,
against-all-odds romances. Eight years ago
she began creating her own characters in
paranormal and time-travel adventures, before
turning to contemporary romance. Other
interests include quilting, astronomy, all things
Scottish and eating anything she doesn't have
to cook. Sharing her characters' journeys with
readers all over the world is a privilege...
and a dream come true. Anne lives in Adelaide,
South Australia, and has two adult children.

Visit her Web site at www.anne-oliver.com.
She loves to hear from readers. E-mail her at
anne@anne-oliver.com.

For my sister, Helen, who now enjoys
Queensland's climate and lifestyle year-round.

With thanks to my editor, Meg Sleightholme.

CHAPTER ONE

ACCORDING to her horoscope, this was Abigail Seymour's lucky day. And with a house named 'Capricorn,' she'd figured she couldn't go wrong.

Wrong.

She stared up at the run-down house from the base of the stairs, comparing it to the photograph in her hand. The weathered board on the veranda trim pronouncing that this was indeed 'Capricorn' hung at a dejected angle and swayed on rusted hinges in the sultry breeze.

In the photograph, the classic Queenslander home stood on stilts for air circulation, enclosed with open lattice-work. Wooden stairs led to a shady wrap-around veranda, which would catch the sea air and provide stunning views of the coastline. Tropical plants added a lush green aspect.

With several coats of paint, some time and energy—correction: a lot of time and energy—it could be that enchanting dwelling once again. She'd be having a few choice words with the agent about false advertising.

Which reminded her—where was he? They'd arranged to meet here this morning. She checked the e-mail printout in her hand, then her watch. A bad feeling cranked up her spine. A very bad feeling. This Gold Coast house was supposed to have been the premises for her new business, Good Vibrations.

At the moment the only vibrations seemed to be coming from somewhere within. And they weren't good. They were the hammering-and-drill-and-not-ready kind. And since she hadn't organised any interior renovations yet… She closed her eyes and took a deep breath. *Think blue, Abby, and calm down.*

Right now it didn't help.

'What the heck's going on?' she muttered. She climbed the stairs, found the front door unlocked and pushed it open.

And stopped in the middle of what looked distressingly like a demolition site. Her fingers clenched around the lease. The signed and dated lease that stated this place was hers from tomorrow.

Wood shavings and lengths of wiring littered the floor. Strips of faded wallpaper hung from one wall above where a large mirror might have hung once upon a time. Dust motes swirled in a thin beam of sunlight and over a wide plank supported by stocky A-frame trestles and covered in tools.

Worse, the place smelled of new wood and old mould, so not the way a massage and aromatherapy centre should smell. Everything was brown and beige and grey.

The usually cheerful jingle of her anklet and beaded sandals sounded out of place on the bare floorboards as she crossed the room. 'Hello?'

No reply. Just the high-pitched whine of a drill.

Picking her way over assorted debris, she skirted the plank table and headed for a door at the back. In the next room a ladder was propped open in a corner near another trestle table. The tinny sound of a transistor radio drifted through the manhole above.

She'd have to settle for grilling the workman. She rapped on the wall. 'Excuse me…?'

The drill reverberated to life again, drowning her voice. Okay, forget the fact that she didn't like heights and that she was trying for a bit of professional decorum here. Setting her bag and papers on the floor, she slipped off her sandals and hitched one side of her skirt under her panty strap.

The loud curse that rolled through the hole was followed by the overhead thump of heavy footsteps. One very bare, well-muscled masculine calf stepped onto the ladder. Then another. Tanned and liberally covered with dark hair. The thighs were no less impressive, and went up and up…until they disappeared beneath brief—and loose-bottomed—denim shorts.

Oh…my. Abby swallowed as those legs descended, followed by one firm, taut backside. She glimpsed a thick ridge of scarring on the back of one thigh disappearing beneath his shorts, then more bare skin, more shifting muscle as his back and a pair of plaster-showered shoulders came into view.

She took an involuntary step back—onto her discarded shoes. The movement caught his attention and the hunk swivelled his head and looked down at her.

Piercing blue eyes met hers. The kind of eyes that looked straight through a woman's clothing and saw her naked. Except this man's eyes never left her face. Still, she had the sensation that he knew exactly what she was wearing right down to her red lace panties.

'Can I help you?' His whisky and sandpaper voice shimmied down Abby's spine like the slow sweep of an exfoliating glove.

She shifted her shoulders inside her T-shirt to ease the tingle. Wiggled her toes back into her sandals. Tugged at her hitched-up skirt and smoothed it down her thigh. She was here on business. He, on the other hand, with his impressive sweat-sheened body and bulging biceps, looked more into brawn than business. More like…a personal trainer?

Her pulse did a little bump. *Blue, blue, blue. Ice-blue. Sky-blue. Lake-blue…like his eyes. Oh, for heaven's sake, get on with it.* 'I'm looking for the owner of this…' She swept an encompassing hand over the clutter.

Lips that were full and sensual and wasted on a man stretched into a smile, creasing his cheeks in a way that made her want to trace the grooves with a finger.

'You found him,' he said, descending the ladder two rungs at a time.

'You?' Mr Tall, Dark and Delicious? She belatedly covered the crack in her voice with a throat-clearing as he approached. Amazing—even at five feet eleven she still had to look up. Early thirties, dark hair, chiselled cheekbones. His slightly off-centre nose was part of the charm.

She wasn't here to be charmed.

Shaking herself into business mode, she retrieved her papers from the floor, straightened her shoulders. 'Mr…'

'Zachary Forrester.' He offered a hand along with another one of those stunning smiles.

Like everything about him, his grip was firm…and tantalisingly brief. But not brief enough for her to miss the sensation of hard, calloused palm against hers. The sparkle of awareness that tingled up her arm.

'Abigail Seymour. Abby. Mr Forrester, I'm…' She trailed off, frowning down at the paper in her hand. Zachary Forrester *wasn't* the name on the lease. She fought a sudden spike of nausea as he grabbed a towel slung on the ladder, swiped it over his sweat-damp hair.

'If you're the insurance rep…' His brow creased as he glanced at her attire.

'Do I look like an insurance rep?' She blew out a breath. 'I'm your new tenant.' She tapped her thigh with the document that proclaimed that fact. 'What's the deal here, Mr Forrester? Because I'm confused.'

His cute dimples winked out and his gaze narrowed. 'That makes two of us. You sure you have the correct address?'

'It says so on that rusted excuse for a mailbox. "Capricorn."' Stepping forward, she shoved the document at his chest—his broad, hairy chest—and caught a whiff of honest-to-goodness male sweat and dust. 'I have a lease for business purposes, starting tomorrow.'

Still frowning, he tossed the towel and reached into the pocket of his shorts, drawing her attention to the way the faded denim… *Keep your eyes above the belt, Abby.* Except he didn't have a belt, and the view above was just as dangerous. Neat little navel, tempting tanned skin… She looked up quickly and saw him slip on a pair of reading glasses.

As he skimmed the paper he raised an eyebrow and one corner of his mouth kicked up. *'Good Vibrations.'*

Abby drew herself up to her full height. Just like a man to take it the wrong way. 'Do you find this funny, Mr Forrester? I assure you, I do not.'

He regarded her over his spectacles, all trace of humour gone. 'Nor do I. This building is a private residence. What kind of business is it exactly…it's *Miss* Seymour, I presume?'

'Yes.' Her hand moved towards her throat as a flush of heat crept up her neck, thanks to the redheads' Curse. 'What are you implying, *exactly*, Mr Forrester? My application was accepted. I have a signed lease to prove it.'

'Not signed by me,' he said over his specs.

'Oh…' She closed her eyes as the lump in her stomach rose to her throat. Was she really standing here letting a sexy stranger witness her business inexpertise?

When she opened them again she was still here and he was still watching her, only now he'd added sympathy and curiosity to the mix.

'I'm sorry, Miss Seymour, but you've been conned.' He tapped the signature with one large blunt finger. 'Not mine. This isn't worth spit. It's not even a legal document.'

If he'd used his hammer, the words couldn't have hit harder. *Not legal.* Her throat constricted. Where had the money for the bond and first three months' hard-earned rent gone? Anger pushed through the emotions swirling through her. 'I signed it in good faith, I *need* this place, and I need it now.'

'How did you find this property?' he said, his attention still focused on the paper in his hand.

'On the Internet. We handled most of the details by e-mail. I had no idea—'

'Obviously.'

She bristled at the know-it-all tone. *Obviously* Zachary Forrester was a lawyer, as well as a handyman. Which had her wondering…how much did lawyers charge?

She wished he'd just hand the paper back and let her go. But, no, he was still reading the fine print. *She* hadn't read the fine print. Who put fine print on an illegal lease anyhow?

Her fingers flexed and curled against her chest. She'd executed the whole deal on her own, not even asked for legal advice. *Stupid.* Aurora would have told her to check it out before putting down her hard-earned cash, and she'd have been right, but she'd wanted to surprise the woman who'd been mother, mentor and friend for the past ten years.

Since her stroke Aurora had been frail, and Abby was

determined to find a place away from rural Victoria's cold, damp climate where she could live out her days in peace. And she'd fallen in love with the picture of the little house…

Now here she was in tropical Surfers Paradise with a phoney lease, a second-hand van of supplies and barely enough money to live on. Talk about Paradise Lost. The deal was also supposed to have included a small self-contained living area so she was now officially homeless, as well.

'Tell me you didn't hand over any money,' Zachary Forrester said, setting his glasses on the trestle.

She bit her lip.

He sighed. A long-drawn-out hiss between his teeth that underscored her own stupidity.

She tried to take the paper but he held it firm, the same way those eyes held hers. 'How much did you give him?' He shook his head. 'We might be able to trace the cheque, I suppose.'

'Um. I paid in cash. In Melbourne. He offered a discount for cash, said he was an agent…'

'Can you describe him? You'll need it when you report the matter to the police.'

'I think so…' Bearded. Blond? Mr Average. She lifted her chin. 'I'm sorry I bothered you, Mr Forrester.'

'Hang on, are you just going to leave it at that and walk away?' He shook his head, incredulous azure eyes searching hers.

'Of course not.' She tugged until the paper slid from his grasp, broke that unnerving eye contact and bent to pick up her bag all in one hurried movement. 'I have your name and address. Count on it, I'll be in touch.'

'What are you going to do?'

'I'm going to report it, then take some time and consider

my options.' *Without you watching,* she thought, sliding the useless document into her bag.

The universe was still out there, she just had to find her place in it. And that place was Queensland's Gold Coast until she sorted out the mess she'd made. Just the thought had her mouth turning as dry as the sand on the nearby shore.

'What options?' His mobile buzzed. He unclipped it from his waistband. 'Forrester. Hi, Tina, honey.' Genuine affection brightened his voice. 'Something came up.' His luscious-looking mouth curved at something Tina Honey said, then he glanced at Abby and it instantly flat-lined as the sparkle in his eyes dimmed. 'No. Nothing like that.' Pause. 'Plenty of time. Yeah. Soon.'

Disconnecting, he clipped the phone in place and said, 'You're not a local, then?'

'No, I arrived from Victoria this morning.' She licked her dried lips, flapped a hand when she saw him frown. 'I'll be fine. My mistake, my problem.'

'Looks like you could do with a drink.' The sandpaper was back in his voice. 'I have a bottle of water in the cooler, or a carton of iced coffee if you prefer.'

Tempting, since she hadn't had anything since her muesli-bar breakfast. But she had more urgent problems than quenching her thirst with an attractive man. This mess wasn't his fault and she'd not involve him any more than she had to. She hitched her bag onto her shoulder. 'Thanks, that's not necessary. And Tina Honey's expecting you.'

A corner of his mouth twitched. 'She's a worrier. It's her son's christening in a couple of hours and I'm the kid's godfather.'

'Congratulations. I'll let you get on with it.'

'Miss Seymour… Abby, we need to discuss this further—'

As he spoke she turned, the sole of her shoe skidded on something, twisting her ankle and sending a shard of pain through her foot. She struggled for balance, her arms pin-wheeled and—

'Whoa there.'

Two hard hands were suddenly supporting her elbows from behind. Embarrassment was stronger than pain as she raised her throbbing foot and glared at the small drill bit on the floor that had caused such an undignified exit. 'This place is a health hazard,' she muttered.

'I'm sorry. I'm renovating on my own— Are you okay?'

As he spoke his breath stirred the hair at her nape, his body heat radiated over her back. And all she could smell was male. Healthy, sweaty male that just begged her female hormones to come out and play. 'It's nothing, I'm fine.' Or she would be if he'd just step away and let her *breathe*.

'Let's take a look.'

'N—'

'Just to be sure.' He cut off her protest as he slid an arm beneath her knees and deposited her on the trestle.

Her feet dangled off the floor—an absolute first. She scoffed to herself. Swept off her feet, the clichéd damsel in distress. Then, with a shifting of shoulder muscles, he hunkered down in front of her and she nearly did the un-appealing swooning bit. Which made her stiffen and straighten up.

'Which foot?' His voice had lowered fractionally.

'It's just a strain. It'll be okay in a couple of minutes—'

'Which foot?' he demanded again.

'Right.'

He slipped off her sandal and cupped her bare foot in one rock-steady hand. Heat spread up her calf as his fingers probed for swelling. The man had the most marvellous touch. Up close, his bent head showed threads of grey amongst the brown.

Of course, he chose that moment to look up. His eyes looked languid, almost silver, but they darkened perceptibly as they met hers.

She looked away. It didn't make a speck of difference. Awareness pumped through her body. Awareness of his hard palm against her heel, his calloused fingertips as they skimmed once over the exquisitely sensitive inside of her ankle.

In the sudden stillness, she could hear her own heart hammering against her breast, the distant sounds of the radio and the waves on the nearby beach. She was having her first—and only—Cinderella moment.

'A gel pack,' he said abruptly. 'There's one in the cooler.'

His clipped no-nonsense voice snapped her back to reality. Time was wasting. Bare-chested hunks masquerading as princes were not on her timetable. 'No, really—'

'Yes, really. I keep it handy just in case.'

He rose, treating her to an eyeful of male crotch. She instantly studied the wall in front of her while he moved to the cooler in the corner.

As a trained remedial massage therapist, she should be used to the sight of the human body. But she wasn't used to the sight of *this* human body. Nor the way it affected her. She felt giddy, breathless, and she straightened her posture again, kept her gaze pinned to the wall.

'Here you go.' He wrapped a cold gel pack around her ankle and held it in place. Thankfully this time his hands didn't stray from the pack.

'Thanks.' She concentrated on visualising a peach-coloured mist around the site of the pain, imagined its healing energies seeping through skin and muscle. But her concentration was shot. Those deft fingers with assorted tiny nicks and scars… Well, they were simply more interesting. She straightened her spine in defiance. *Close your eyes, Abigail Seymour.*

Zak felt like a damn Prince Charming. Except that after a brief but necessary probe for swelling—he didn't need a lawsuit on his hands—this prince was keeping his fingers well away from that feminine ankle with its erotic silver anklet.

Abigail Seymour was *not* his ideal princess.

She'd knocked him off-beam when he'd first laid eyes on her only because he hadn't expected to see a spectacularly tall, red-haired female ogling his backside when he descended the ladder.

His gaze flicked to her face. Now she seemed to be locked in some sort of introspection. He already knew behind those closed lids her eyes were a misty grey. Like the ocean when a storm rolled in.

He wondered how they'd look glazed with passion.

And why had that particular image popped into his head? Because he hadn't indulged in that pastime in a long while, that was why. He knew the old saying: all work and no play…

He shook his head and rocked back on his heels, careful to keep his fingers at a constant pressure so as not to disturb her internal focus…and—turnabout was fair play—ogled her back.

She dressed like a seventies cast-off, and this morning's colour scheme seemed to be all about intensity—purple-on-magenta skirt and crimson top. She'd made some attempt to tame her red hair, which was pulled into a tight knot at her nape, but a few strands had worked loose and the whole lot looked as if it might rebel given the least opportunity.

Freckles dotted her nose and cheeks. Minimal make-up, a hint of soap overlaid by something more exotic. Some sort of mysterious floral essence? Incense? She wore a trio of silver rings on the fingers of her right hand. An aquamarine was suspended on a chain around her neck.

As if she felt his scrutiny, she opened her eyes. 'That'll do.'

She jerked her foot but he held it firm, his fingers briefly straying beyond the pack. 'Better safe than sorry. A couple more minutes. Isn't Victoria a long way to come to start a business?'

'When you want something, my motto is go out and get it… I guess it's not always as easy as you think it's going to be.' She shrugged a shoulder, giving him a peek of red lace bra strap.

The sight had his blood pumping a little faster through his veins. He almost laughed aloud. He'd definitely been out of circulation a long time if a bra strap turned him on.

What *did* she want? Just a business? She could do that in Melbourne. A tropical lifestyle, then? A sea change?

Or a torrid affair.

He cleared a sudden tightness from his throat. 'So, you owned a business in Melbourne?'

'Not exactly.' She shifted uneasily on the trestle. 'Mr Forrester—'

'Zak. What's that supposed to mean: "not exactly"?'

'I was involved in someone else's business. Don't worry, I know what I'm doing.'

Debatable, he thought as she pulled her foot from his grasp as if she couldn't wait to get away.

'You'll be late for Tina and I need to be going.'

'We're not finished…but it'll have to wait,' he said,

glancing at his watch. He set the pack on the trestle, slipped her sandal on.

As he closed his hands around the slender curve of her waist to deposit her on the floor a wariness flashed into her eyes and she raised both palms. 'I can manage, thanks.'

Her body remained as stiff as a patio post but her hands rose unwillingly to his shoulders as she slid off the trestle. He swore he felt each finger, a pressure point of what he refused to call pleasure. Pleasure was something he had no business feeling. Ever again.

The moment her feet hit the floor he stepped back. 'Where are you staying?' He heard the brusqueness in his voice. 'I need to be able to contact you. In case any information comes to light.'

Which it wouldn't. The low-life responsible had stolen her money and disappeared into cyber space long ago. It made Zak angry. Especially when he saw the spark of hope in her eyes as she gazed up at him.

'You think it might?'

'No.' He felt sorry for it, but that was the bare truth. 'And I want a photocopy of that lease.'

'Why?'

'You don't think I should have a copy of something involving my own property?'

She blinked as if the logic had just occurred to her. 'Of course you should.' She dug into her bag and pulled out a fancy feminine-looking pad and pen. She scribbled something, ripped off the sheet. 'My mobile number. You can contact me on that.'

Keeping his eyes focused on hers, he ripped off the bottom half. 'Don't you want mine?' He took her pen, warm from her fingers, wrote his number and handed both back. Then he pulled his wallet from his back pocket and withdrew a couple of business cards. 'In case you have any problems.' A foregone conclusion.

She glanced at the cards. '"Forrester Building Restorations" and "Capricorn Centre"?' Her eyes twinkled as she smiled at him for the first time. 'You're a busy boy, Mr Forrester. Do you make any time in your schedule for fun?'

His jaw tightened. He preferred it when she wasn't smiling. Fun with Abigail Seymour conjured disturbingly uncomfortable images. 'If my mobile's not switched on you can contact me through the centre's office.'

'O-kay.' She tucked them in her bag while he filed her info in his pocket.

He saw her wince on that first step as she accompanied him through the front room and out into the balmy ocean air. Beyond the fence he saw the beat-up van with Victorian licence plates and shook his head in disbelief. 'You drove all the way in that? Alone?'

She dug out her keys with a jumble of colourful crystals and whatnots attached to the ring. 'You wouldn't?'

'Not a chance.'

'Some of us don't have the luxury of that choice. Scrappy here's good for a few thousand ks yet.'

While he stared, still shaking his head, she patted it fondly, then climbed in.

He refused to acknowledge whatever the hell it was that hummed through his body as her exotic fragrance wound its way through his senses, at the sound of her anklet tinkling as she swung her legs beneath the steering column. As her eyes met his through the car's open window.

'I'll call you,' Zak heard himself say, and was suddenly conscious of his choice of words. 'Later,' he added. 'Contact me if you need anything in the meantime.'

He shut the door and watched the car chug off in a cloud of fumes. *Some of us don't have a choice.* She didn't deserve the low blow she'd been dealt. Brought about by her own carelessness, he reminded himself. He rolled his eyes to the tropical blue sky. How naïve could the woman be? To put down money without checking first—a more cynical guy might say she deserved what had happened to her. She wouldn't be so quick and trusting the next time.

He walked back inside and immediately headed for the cooler. Opened a bottle of water, gulped it down, then looked at the mess. He didn't even know what kind of business she'd wanted to set up—she'd sneakily let that question slide.

It wasn't his fault. *Don't get involved.* But, damn it, he *was* involved—it was his property after all—which meant giving her a call later, as he'd told her he would. See if he could help. Get a photocopy of her document.

He reached into his pocket and pulled out the piece of paper she'd given him. Her scent wafted to his nose as he unfolded it. A bold, flourishing *A* for Abby. One of those smiley faces at the bottom, and an *X*. His brow lifted. Presumably she ended all her correspondence in that carefree upbeat manner.

Would she make love the same way? With a snarl he shoved away thoughts and images that crept into his brain and edged dangerously close to desire. She was nothing like his kind of woman. Nothing like Diane. So there was *nothing* to worry about.

CHAPTER TWO

'WHERE have you been?' Tina Hammond demanded at the church door. 'And smelling…' Her classic patrician nose wrinkled as if she couldn't decide, then she arched her brows. 'Mmm. Exotic. What *is* that scent?'

Ignoring her scrutiny, Zak bent to kiss her forehead. 'Careful, you're starting to sound like a wife.'

She grinned, patted his cheek. 'Just trying it on for practice. Not long now.'

'You do realise you guys have the ceremonies back to front, don't you?'

'It just worked out that way.' Tina's blue silk dress rustled as she reached up to adjust his tie. The familiar feminine gesture and fussy sound she made as she smoothed his lapel was something he'd not been subjected to in a long while.

'We want to say our "I do's" on that island, even if we've had to wait a year for the booking.' Her dark eyes zeroed in on his with unsettling directness. 'Are you bringing the wearer of that perfume to the wedding?'

'Good grief, no.'

She cocked that little blond head of hers to one side, her eyes soft with sympathy and understanding. 'You haven't asked anyone, have you? I told you, I can arrange for a partner—'

'Not necessary.' Zak squeezed her hands briefly before setting her away and buttoned his suit jacket. He forced himself to put aside his misgivings about being surrounded by so many well-meaning friends when he'd prefer solitude and took a deep breath. 'Now, where's that godson of mine?'

'Nick's got him.' Tucking her arm in Zak's, she towed him down the aisle to her soon-to-be husband and the wide-eyed Daniel nestled in his arms.

Zak exchanged greetings, spoke briefly to the grandparents, skimmed a hand over the eight-month-old's silky head, then took his place alongside the family.

As the minister led the brief service Zak couldn't stop the memories of that day six years ago when he'd stood here in the emerald and sapphire and gold light filtering through that stained glass and made his marriage vows.

Tina was so similar to Diane, both petite blondes, well educated and fashion savvy. The three of them had been inseparable right through school, but it had been Diane who'd won his heart as childhood matured into adolescence and adulthood.

Tina worked four days a week in Zak's new office but Zak knew that these days her greatest love was being a mother. And now Diane had gone, that instinctive mothering seemed to extend to Zak.

He shifted restlessly in the pew as the minister droned on about family. He dreaded these social gatherings. The awkward silences. The consoling hand on his, the dinner invites. But this was one gathering he couldn't avoid.

Almost the entire assembled congregation knew him. Had known his wife. They knew he'd nearly lost his own life alongside her.

They didn't know of his nightmares, or the guilt that stalked him at every turn.

Because they didn't know the whole story…

'You weren't alone in that Singapore hotel room,' he accused Diane the moment he saw her an hour after she'd flown in on that last buying trip to Asia. He hadn't waited until they had privacy; no, he'd had to confront her at their friend's birthday bash. Mistake number one.

She'd only just turned up and they were by the front gate, the night cool and awash with purple shadows and bougainvillea.

'Nor did you tell me your flight arrival time,' he continued. 'Did he fly in with you? Is he a local? Do I know him?'

'You're being paranoid,' she said. But her eyes skittered away and she flitted past him, already smelling of booze.

'No. I'm not.' He grabbed her arm. 'I'm taking you home. We need to sort this out.'

'Let me go.'

'Okay, since you're so insistent.' But he hesitated, his fingers pressing into her flesh. 'If you're not going to come clean, this marriage is over.' The silence in that brief hiatus as the meaning sank in, for both of them, sounded like a gunshot. 'But I'm still taking you home.'

'I didn't tell you my flight because I didn't want you to miss the party.'

'Yeah, right.'

Her face was pale in the dimness, her eyes huge and moist. 'You've got it wrong. It was the TV you could hear…'

Right now all he could hear was his own heart pounding with fear. His gut cramped, his facial muscles twitched with strain. 'I'm not a fool.'

Mistake number two was letting go of her to dig in his pocket for his car keys, then dropping them in the low broad-leafed bushes that edged the lawn.

When he reached the kerb she was already gone, her car fishtailing as it veered left onto the main road.

He caught up with her a kilometre away and stayed with her for twenty minutes as she headed west towards the hinterland, cursing her, cursing himself a hundred times over. Then they reached the bridge…

Too late to listen to her side, to find out if he'd been wrong. God forbid, horribly wrong. Too damn late.

'Zak?' Nudging him out of his past, Tina whispered into his ear, 'You're supposed to stand now.'

He nodded, rose, rolled the kinks from his shoulders all in one movement. 'Sorry.' And hoped he'd make a better godfather than he had a husband.

'So, how are the renovations coming?' Nick Langotti asked, jostling his son on his hip. The christening was being followed by a lavish afternoon tea on Nick and Tina's palm-shaded patio.

Until a few weeks ago Zak had been occupying a room in the apartment building he'd bought soon after Diane's death last year while Forrester Building Restorations oversaw the renovations to turn it into a tourist and conference centre.

Zak popped the top on a can of beer. 'Kitchen's looking good and I've finished the two bedrooms and *en suite* bathroom. The rest of the place is still a war zone.' He selected a few slices of salami and cheese and put them on his plate. 'It's taking a backseat until Capricorn Centre's more established. And I still have that empty retail space to rent out there.'

'You still going with that ad campaign the agency suggested?'

'If I can find a suitable model.' The Face of Capricorn. Someone able to project the image of a professional who could have fun when lectures were finished for the day. 'I've got an appointment at a photographic model agency tomorrow to look through their books,' Zak said.

Nick's eyebrows jiggled. 'You want me to come with you and help check them out?'

'Help check who out?' With the unerring sense that wives—even soon-to-be ones—seemed to develop whenever a topic specific to the female gender came up, Tina materialised at Nick's side. She was licking cream from her index finger and eyeing Zak with that look he'd come to recognise as some sort of futile hope. 'Anyone I know?'

Time to leave, Zak decided, before anyone else got it into their head to offer him tea and sympathy.

And the thirty-minute walk home would clear his head. It was also the best way to avoid chauffeuring any of Tina's girl-friends who just happened to need a lift home.

'Had a few too many vinos, Te-e-na, I'm over the limit,' he told her with an exaggerated drawl before leaving his car in their driveway to pick up later.

Desperate for some fresh sea air and solitude, he headed straight for the esplanade. He tugged off his tie, slipped it in his pocket and undid the top couple of buttons of his shirt.

Being surrounded by all that family—its noise and laughter and love—reminded him of what he didn't have. His place didn't have cosmetics strewn over the vanity, a jar of home-made cookies on the kitchen bench, diapers airing under the veranda. Not that Diane had been the domestic sort. She'd worked long hours to get ahead in her job, which had left little time for anything else.

At present his kitchen table was home to assorted hardware rather than fresh flowers and the only cookies were store-bought and eaten straight from the packet, usually a month after the use-by date.

He realised he'd reached the esplanade and was standing on the beach—in his formals, for crying out loud. He watched the sky, lavender with early twilight, listened to the sound of the waves, a rhythmic shushing on the sand.

Then everything inside him stilled and tensed as his eyes focused on the view directly in front of him.

And what a view it was. Not the white sand or the turquoise water turning cobalt as the sun dropped below the high-rise apartment blocks behind him.

The woman. The don't-give-a-damn-who's-watching, living-life-and-loving-it woman.

A silver-spangled violet and blue skirt flared around her bare feet, revealing that she was indeed human and not a mermaid. The beaded turquoise top and the long rainbow scarf tied around her slim waist were pure gypsy.

Then she glanced over her shoulder, an innocently seductive movement that had Zak freezing to the spot, his breath backing up in his lungs.

Abigail Seymour.

She'd let her hair down—and how. Yards and yards of deep red spirals whirled behind her in the stiff breeze like a celebration of streamers at a New Year's Eve party. She raised a hand and ran her fingers through it.

He exhaled slowly, his blood hammering hot and fast through his veins. He clenched his suddenly tight jaw. His first thought was to avoid her at all costs. He should just turn and walk away. Go home. Take a cold shower. He didn't want the distraction of that image keeping him awake tonight. Or any night.

More disturbing, the sight of Diane had never stirred his body the way Abigail Seymour was doing.

While his feet were still getting the message from his brain, which had suddenly seized up, she flirted with the water's edge again. Her skirt had soaked water up to her knees. Did she even care that other beach-goers enjoying their sunset stroll were slowing down to witness the spectacle of an almost six-foot redhead darting in and out of the waves as if she were performing some kind of dance?

She was a natural. A stunning contrast of curves and colours against the stark linear skyscrapers behind her, her shoulders catching the afterglow of sunset.

A light-bulb moment.

He barely noticed he'd started walking again. Capricorn had a face. It had a body. No model the agency could throw at him would come close. He was prepared to do whatever it took to get her. And that included getting his expensive Italian shoes wet.

In his mind's eye he could already picture her long slim body reclining on the bed in one of his centre's deluxe suites, that spectacular hair spread out on the pillow. A silk negligee clinging to her curves… Even from several steps away he could smell her scent mingling with the tang of salt and sand.

Abby let the sand squish between her toes as she walked along the ocean's edge. Water always relieved her stress; the sign of a true Piscean. She'd wasted time in an Internet café trying to trace a false name and her money. She'd also looked up Forrester Building Restorations and Capricorn Centre to satisfy herself that Zak was who he claimed to be at the same time.

He was. And, from the glowing reports of satisfied

clients and the photos of his work, he was very success-ful. And she'd found a place to stay within her tight budget, so it hadn't all been a wasted effort.

But another interesting tidbit she'd discovered was that Capricorn Centre had business premises to rent, a topic she intended bringing up when she saw him again.

'Abby, wait up!'

Her breath caught in her throat at the familiar sound of that deep-timbred voice. How long had Zak Forrester been watching her cavort in the waves like a regular sea nymph? She turned to see him striding across the sand towards her. In his pressed charcoal trousers and shiny shoes he looked like the self-made success her research had uncovered.

She almost smiled as she watched the lacy edge of the sea foam splash those shiny shoes. If she'd been worried about what he'd make of her little dance, she needn't be; he looked as out of his depth as she.

'Abby.' He stopped a few feet away. 'First up, have you been to the cops?'

'Yes. I gave them a statement.' *For all the good it will do.*

He nodded, then said, 'I have a proposition for you.'

Her face and neck prickled. *'Proposition?'*

'How would you like to make up the money you've lost? Give yourself some breathing space till you find something suitable.' So he'd witnessed her few moments of impulsive abandon—she should be much more con-cerned that the Hunk was a Sleaze. But his eyes weren't sleazy—just a hot lightning blue that zinged through her body like an electric current.

Shocked at her response, she took a step back. 'And that would be dependent on…?'

'A favour.'

A laugh scraped up her dry throat and escaped. 'Is that one step up or down from a proposition?'

'You can tell me.' Intense blue eyes assessed her, from the tips of her flyaway hair to her purple lacquered toenails, then back to her eyes. 'Let's negotiate something over coffee or a snack. Have you had dinner?'

Her stomach rumbled on cue. 'No.'

'Okay. I know a place.'

Still unsure whether his so-called proposition was a good idea, she asked, 'Is this dinner strictly business or is it personal?'

His gaze wavered a moment before he said, 'Call it an interview in casual surroundings. You can think about my suggestion and maybe I can help you find other premises afterwards. I'll explain my idea and you could explain your Mission Statement.' He stared down at her. 'You do have one, don't you?'

Was that a hint of humour in his eyes? She couldn't be sure. 'Doesn't everyone?'

Of course she had a…Mission Statement. Somewhere. If only she knew what the heck hers was. If only she knew whether he was serious.

She strode past him and across the sand, collected her bag and towel. When she began securing her scrunchie around her hair, he stopped her with a hand on her wrist. Heat zinged up her arm and through her body.

'Leave it.' Then as suddenly as he touched her, his hand dropped away as if he instantly regretted it and his jaw tightened.

'Fine, if you want to share a table with Miz Frizz,' she said, rubbing the spot on her hand that still tingled. Had she imagined the sparks? She shoved the scrunchie into her bag, her taste buds dancing in anticipation of sustenance. 'You promised food.'

'I did,' Zak said, behind her. 'Simon Says has the best-value steaks in town.'

'Oh, before we go any further…' She spun around, her arm brushing against the smooth body-warmed fabric of his shirt in the process, and held up a hand '…so there's no misunderstanding, is there a Mrs Forrester, or someone of the female gender you need to call and explain why you're going to be late?'

She saw the flicker in the depths of his eyes, heard the hesitation in his voice before he said, 'No.'

His shuttered expression forestalled any elaboration. She hadn't had lunch and the offer of a free meal was too tempting to resist. She nodded and headed for the line of parked cars.

'Only one small problem,' he said when they reached the kerb. 'I walked to the beach. Can you give me a lift?'

She couldn't resist a certain smugness. 'Would that be in my beat-up van that's brought me all the way across the country?'

His dimples creased as he smiled. 'That's the one.'

Her heart skipped a beat. Oh, boy. Dimples did it for her every time. But how well did she know this guy? This sexy *single* guy.

Sometimes you had to go with your gut feeling—she felt safe with Zak Forrester. If you didn't count the dangerous spark of excitement in her bloodstream whenever she looked at him. But she was at the wheel and in control and she didn't have to go anywhere she didn't want.

'No out-of-the-way restaurants,' she warned. Unlocking the door, she tossed her stuff in the back, cleared off the passenger seat and wound down the window. The van still smelled of last night's less-than-healthy but quick chicken burger and fries.

As he climbed in he cast a questioning glance at her precious supplies on the backseat and rear. Boxes stacked on boxes, a couple of cases and a mountain of bulging plastic garbage bags.

Ignoring his curiosity, she strapped in and turned on the ignition. Her bare foot tapped the accelerator. 'All in good time, Mr Forrester.'

Zak directed Abby to his favourite eatery overlooking the esplanade where the food came fast, was well prepared and inexpensive.

But it wasn't the ocean view that had Zak's attention tonight. It was Abby. The damp hem of her skirt and bare feet suited the casual atmosphere. His wife would have been appalled, hence he'd never come here unless he'd been alone. Diane had never stepped outside without high heels and make-up, but on Abby it looked right.

Diners lingered over their ice-cream sundaes or mango delights in shorts and beach wraps. In his blinding white shirt sleeves and formal trousers, *he* was the one out of dress code.

'What appeals to your taste buds?' he asked when Paul appeared at their table. He knew what appealed to his own right now and it wasn't on the menu. Had he made a mistake bringing her out to eat, when a nice safe coffee at the office would have served the same purpose?

She looked up at him with those luminous grey eyes. *Yeah, big mistake.*

'I'll have the seafood linguini, please,' she said.

'Wine?'

'Just a glass of hot water with a teaspoon of apple cider

vinegar and one of honey…You can do that, right?' she asked Paul.

'Of course,' he said, without a flicker of surprise, while Zak felt his own eyebrows lift. 'I'll have the fillet steak, rare, with a side serve of vegetables, please, and a beer.' He set the menu aside. 'An interesting choice of beverage.'

'A natural feel-good tonic. After today I need an extra boost. I take it twice a day, that's how I stay balanced.'

He toyed with the salt and pepper shakers. Balanced: two perfect eyes, perfectly aligned shoulders… But that was symmetrical, not balanced… A pair of firm breasts resting like half moons on her folded arms as she studied the decor. She was in perfect shape…ah…balance.

She turned her head and caught him looking. In the long pause he was aware of the muted sounds of a CD playing a Hawaiian love song, the ocean's roll, snatches of other diners' conversations.

'Whereas you…' She stared at him. Not *at* him, but around him. He had to force himself not to turn his head. 'You need to change the colour of your bedroom,' she said, without a glimmer of humour. 'You suffer from insomnia and recurring lower back pain.'

A tingle sprinted down his spine. Only his physician knew about the pain he'd suffered since the accident and the nightmares that plagued him. He wanted to test Abby's theory. He wanted to take her to his bedroom and ask her decorating advice. See if she could give him some personal help with his insomnia. And his lower back.

Hell. He shifted on his chair, cracked his knuckles. What was happening to him? 'That's not caused by my choice of interior decorating. It's the stress of renovating my home while splitting my time between two businesses. And I lift heavy equipment for a living.'

Her gaze dropped to the open neck of his shirt. 'Tell me about it.'

His skin tightened at her intimate invitation and a spike of adrenaline stabbed through his body.

'Conferences and tourism, wasn't it?' she said, grinding his wrongly interpreted thoughts to dust. 'Where do I fit in?'

Their drinks came at that moment with a basket of fragrant hot rolls. He took a gulp of beer to moisten his mouth. 'Okay. Here's what I'm offering. The centre needs a promotion to really get it up and running. I'd like to use you.'

She took a long sip of her beverage, her eyes wary. 'How do you propose to do that?'

'We'd employ a professional photographer. Some shots of you on the beach in—' his gaze slid to her visible top half '—something like what you're wearing now.' He forced his eyes to hers. 'And maybe a bathing costume, another of you in conference mode… A business suit…?'

She didn't smile as he'd hoped. 'I don't own one.'

'Not a problem, we'll get you one. I'll pay for the necessary clothes. Think about it, Abby. I'm offering to recompense you for your loss in exchange for a couple of hours of easy work.'

Her brows lowered, and he could almost hear her mind working over his suggestion.

He pressed on. 'We'll take a look at where I intend to shoot it and you can give it some thought. Throw in a beauty makeover, new wardrobe, whatever you want—'

'I'm comfortable with the way I look, thanks.' Her eyes cooled, her lips pursed. 'And dress.'

'Of course. You look great the way you are, which is why I want you. For the promotion.' Crikey, he was negotiating a high beam here with one foot in his mouth.

She lifted her glass again. 'I don't want payment. I want first option on the empty retail space you're advertising.'

He jerked upright. Out of the question. He knew next to nothing about her or her business. And how the devil did she know?

She tipped her glass towards him. 'I saw it on the Internet.'

'I'm considering another tenant,' he lied. 'And since you haven't mentioned the nature of your business—'

'I'm a remedial massage therapist. Just the thing your centre needs. I look forward to seeing it.' She settled back comfortably. 'Ever had your horoscope charted?' she asked suddenly, jerking his attention in another direction. 'By the way, your star sign's Taurus.' She opened her roll and buttered it.

His own bread lodged behind his Adam's apple. 'You believe in that stuff?' The fact that she had him pegged so neatly was as unnerving as it was fluky.

She smiled that knowing smile that raised the hairs on the back of his neck and tapped a finger on the table. 'You're grounded, Zak, and you don't like change. You like the sensual things in life. The massage thing appeals to you, I saw it in your eyes. You're also practical so you're wondering if you should take a chance on an unknown girl who's a little too alternative for you.' She paused. 'How am I doing so far?'

You're a good people-reader, that's all. 'That doesn't mean I fit into a mould created by the position of a bunch of stars in the sky.'

'You own a house and a centre named after a zodiacal sign—keep an open mind.' She licked a smidgen of butter off her thumb. 'But I'll forgive you, because a Taurean is also a fixed sign and stubborn into the bargain.'

'You could be right. Because I'll tell you now, this stubborn Taurean doesn't give up easily.'

'Good for you.' She pinned him with an equally obstinate gaze. 'But if you don't agree to my suggestion, it's a moot trait.'

Their meal came, a rather silent affair because Abby seemed more interested in food right now and he had to wonder when she'd last had a decent meal, given her circumstances.

He waited until she'd scraped the last morsel from her plate, then said, 'Tell me more about your business.'

'Ah, that would mean my, um…*Mission Statement*, I assume?' Her brow wrinkled in thought. 'Good Vibrations offers a holistic approach. A balm for body, mind and spirit. To this end, I also include aromatherapy and music in my sessions. Because I believe the whole experience is governed by the mood created by the surroundings, I'd also like to have the final say in the colour scheme.'

What? 'Wait up—'

'Let me finish.' She tapped a purple fingernail on the table between them. 'Colour affects the environment and our moods.' She looked about her. 'This café, for instance. The red cloths and warm honey wood give a feeling of welcome. The windows, open to the green of the palms and the blue of the sea, invite relaxation. Agreed?'

He leaned back in his chair, prepared to listen, at least. 'Go on.'

'Colour's invisible vibrations help us in our lives. Good Vibrations will treat clients to all aspects of relaxation and incorporate services which indulge or soothe the senses, such as aromatherapy and massage.' She smiled as she rolled her napkin between her fingers, excitement dancing over her features. 'I'm told my massage technique is magic. Just think, I could cater to tourists and conference attendees after a long hard day of playing or conferring.'

He *was* thinking, but for a moment he was lost in the way her eyes lit up as she talked, the sparkle of enthusiasm in her voice. He was thinking how her oiled hands would feel sliding over his scarred lower back… He shifted inside his shirt. And he couldn't avoid the clench of his body whenever she lifted a shoulder in that fascinating way she had.

But guests would take advantage of a service like massage or aromatherapy, particularly if it was right in the centre itself. 'It could work. But the rental on a place like this doesn't come cheap.'

'Neither do my massages.' Her smile was wicked as she leaned down to collect her bag. 'Let's go.'

Heat smoked and curled deep in his gut. The air in his lungs thickened. He clenched his hands into fists on his knees, willing his reaction away. *No*. But denial laughed at him and the aching loneliness of losing Diane, the absence of a woman's touch in over a year, blazed to hot and hungry life.

By the time he shook away the red haze from his vision he realised she'd hitched her bag onto her shoulder and without a backward glance was walking to the door.

He watched her while he dug out his wallet. This meal had been *business*, he reminded himself. As was his relationship with Miss Abigail Seymour.

So why was he still sitting here with his eyes glued to the sway of her backside, the long, long length of her legs silhouetted against the sheer fabric of her skirt, and wondering what colour negligee would suit her best?

Damnation. He dragged his gaze away, pulled out his credit card and slapped it against his palm. He should have gone for a professional model as he'd intended. Now he had to be on hand for the photographs. He had to make decisions about how best to clothe—or unclothe—that body.

His mouth dried and his body spiked with a sexual energy that jolted him from head to toe. What the hell had he got himself into?

CHAPTER THREE

ZAK'S voice turned all clipped and businesslike as he directed her to the centre. Abby didn't spare him a glance; she didn't need the distraction. With the van's windows down, the breeze caught her hair, tossing it every which way.

To ease the tension that had sprung up between them, she flicked the radio on to a local station and concentrated on the scenery. It was full dark and an old gold moon was rising over the Pacific. Architecturally diverse skyscrapers she'd never seen the likes of in her part of the world slid by. A fairy-tale land of twinkling lights and holiday-makers.

But this was no fairy tale, Zak was no prince and she needed these premises.

'This is it.' Zak indicated a white building with jutting balconies on the upper floors. Lights shone through a few windows.

'Wow.' She braked in the driveway for a better look as excitement buzzed through her veins.

'The centre's open but we're just getting started,' he explained.

Setting the van into motion again, she continued up the circular drive lined with pandanus and bright hibiscus bushes and, at his direction, parked under a covered portico, then gazed up at the shiny bronze lettering. 'Capricorn Centre.' Its unique angles and architectural charm were as clear as day in the floodlights illuminating the building.

A row of old pines separated the centre from an expanse of sand covered in sea grasses, and beyond she could see the white scrolls of surf glittering in the moonlight.

They climbed out at the same time and walked to the glassed entrance. A chandelier's light flooded the lobby. She instantly approved the colour scheme: a basic warm cream with splashes of emerald green and rose in the up-holstery and furnishings, the gleaming wooden floor and banisters on the staircase that led upstairs. Mirrors re-flected the lights and added a sense of space.

She caught a whiff of Zak's cologne—something cool and green—as they crossed the marbled floor. She was going to smell that scent in her sleep—if she got any sleep. Her mind was ticking over at a hundred miles an hour.

'The ground floor's admin and shopping, conference rooms and dining. The upper two are bedrooms. It's not large, but I didn't want large. I was going for exclusive.'

'So where's the room I'll be most interested in?'

'Over here.' He led her down a wide hallway and un-locked a double-glass door. Through the window on the far side she glimpsed the sea through the pines before he switched on the subtle lighting.

Oh, my… She drank in the pastel-blue walls, the deeper blue flecked with plum in the wall-to-wall carpet. 'Your interior decorator knew what they were doing.' She couldn't have chosen better herself. 'I'll need a privacy screen and maybe a little tabletop fountain there…' She reined in her runaway enthusiasm. She had to fulfil her side of the bargain first. *And* get him to agree to rent it to her.

He walked to the window and stood, shoulders tense, hands on his hips; a lengthy pause while he watched the moon reflecting on the water, obviously grappling with some inner conflict. 'Do you come with any testimonials from satisfied clients?' he said. '*If* I agree to this, I'll need to be able to recommend your services to our guests.'

'I do. But you and your staff will each receive a complimentary session. We can schedule yours as soon as I've set up.'

His hands clenched. 'That won't be necessary.'

'From where I'm standing it sure looks like you could do with one.'

She watched his shoulders hunch further. 'Very well,' he said finally. 'A rent-free three-month trial. In return for a series of professional photographs to be used for promotional purposes only…and all expenses incurred—the outfits you'll wear—to be covered by me.'

Yes! Because he had his back to her, she punched one fist into the air and yelled a silent *hallelujah*! 'You won't be sorry.'

'What about a massage bed?' His voice dropped a notch on the last two words, and he seemed to be having trouble with the imagery because he waved a disconcerted hand, then ran it around the inside of his collar as he turned.

'I don't need one. I prefer working on the floor.' And despite her best professional intentions, she couldn't prevent her own images of a naked Zak Forrester and heat and hands and fragrant oil from creeping into her consciousness. Not professional at all.

His eyes darkened to indigo, and a muscle jumped in his jaw. 'I'll supply shelving, anything else you provide yourself.'

'Fine. Oh, and I want it in writing first.'

He nodded, moved to the middle of the room. 'Pleased

to see you're being careful. I'll have it drawn up and bring it over… You haven't told me where you're staying.'

'No. I didn't.' Nor did she intend to. He didn't quite believe her; she could tell by the crease between his brows. 'I'll be here tomorrow.' She held his gaze. 'Trust me, Zak, I'll be here. It started out such a horrible day, and now…' She crossed the space between them. 'Thank you.' And threw her arms around his neck and planted a purely innocent lip-smacking kiss on his mouth.

But there was nothing pure, or innocent, about the way her body responded. Her lips buzzed, burned. Every internal organ seemed to trade places. Her arms turned as limp as the linguini she'd eaten for dinner, sliding off his shoulders and down his chest, the weave of his shirt soft against her fingers as she leaned back to stare up at him. At that mouth.

As his hands splayed around her waist. As he leaned forward, just a little… To kiss her again?

No. To steady her—she was the one swaying.

His mouth didn't look at all pleased. 'Are you always so enthusiastic about everything?' it said tersely, his hands dropping away to fist at his sides. But the heat in his eyes said something entirely different.

'I'm afraid so. Sorry.' She backed away on wobbly legs. Oh, that mouth was a temptation. 'Let's…um…sleep on it. You look like you could do with some.'

He didn't respond, but his eyes darkened with some unidentifiable emotion as she turned. She could feel those eyes on her as they tracked her progress to the door.

'Try some chamomile tea,' she suggested as she turned to him in the doorway. 'On second thought…your lower-back pain?' She hadn't meant to say it, but a sudden image of her hands working over his back, her thumbs digging into the taut muscles of his buttocks—*without* the clothes—and finding all those secret, sensitive places…' Better make that valerian.'

Abby pulled up at her unpowered site in the caravan park she'd booked earlier in the day. She switched off the ignition. 'Welcome to your new home, Abby,' she said, staring up at the nearby holiday apartments lighting the night sky and wishing she were cosying up in one of those luxury beds.

Instead, she was slap bang in the middle of Surfers without any kind of a bed and no electricity.

But once the deal was signed, she could offload her supplies and sleep in the back of the van. Not an ideal situation but she could make do.

She speed-dialled Aurora's number on her mobile. Guilt niggled at her, but she'd put off calling today hoping she'd have better news or at least some concrete information.

The familiar voice at the other end brought a lump of homesickness to her throat. Aurora meant more to Abby than anyone in the world. When she and her husband, Bill, had fostered the rebellious sixteen-year-old ten years ago, Abby had had no idea how her life would turn around.

She pressed the phone closer to her ear, wishing she were there. Wishing she hadn't rushed into something without discussing it with Aurora first. 'Hi, Rory, it's me.'

'Abby, thank goodness. I've been worried. When you didn't call…'

'I've been busy today. First up, how are you feeling? Is the career working out?'

'Fine to both questions. How's everything at your end? Did you get the job you were hoping for?'

'I did.' She injected a smile into her voice at the small

lie. 'It's in a new conference centre. Get this, Rory, it's called Capricorn. It has loads of potential.'

Abby hadn't told Aurora the truth when she'd left—that she'd wanted to set up her own business. That she'd hoped to be able to bring her here as soon as she had it up and running.

'Capricorn? Well, that's a good sign if ever there was one.' There was a pause, then she said, 'I know you have your own life now, but perhaps I can come up when I'm feeling better, and stay with you a while.'

Abby heard the wistful tone in Aurora's voice. She missed her already. She *hated* letting her think she'd taken a job in Queensland for the fun of it, especially so soon after Aurora's stroke. But if she told her the truth and what a mess she'd made of everything, Aurora would worry and insist on helping her out financially, and Abby refused to allow that to happen. She owed her foster mum, not the other way round.

She dashed the moisture from her eyes. 'It won't be for ever, Rory. Just until I get my feet on the ground, then I'll get you up here.'

'Of course, love. Who's your boss, what's he like and what's his star sign?'

Boss. The nearest she had to a boss was…Zak. Abby's heart skipped a beat as the man who'd put her hormones on alert came to Technicolor life behind her eyes. She could still smell his cologne in the car, could still feel the tingle of his lips on hers. 'His name's Zak Forrester and he's a Taurean.'

'Ah-h-h…'

Abby frowned at the tone, as if all the mysteries in the world were solved. '*Ah*…what?'

'Nothing, love. He's a hard worker, that's all-practical, and don't forget obstinate.'

Don't forget tall. Gorgeous. Sex god. 'Obstinate, indeed,' Abby agreed, 'particularly when it comes to alternative beliefs and practices.' And over-enthusiastic redheads.

'Don't let him intimidate you.'

She almost laughed. She'd been the one who'd intimidated *him.* 'I won't. Keep safe, I'll ring you tomorrow.'

Abby didn't see the sun's watery ascent over the sea, but she felt its tentacles as they crept over the dashboard, peeling her eyelids back just when she'd finally managed to snatch a couple of hours' sleep. Her neck ached from being propped against the van's door. Everything ached, she discovered as she dragged the hair out of her eyes and pushed upright. Stretching out the kinks, she took in her new surroundings.

Instead of the sound of eucalypts tossed by winter winds, palm fronds slapped languidly against each other. Children were already splashing in the park's pool. And some sadist was cooking bacon. She sucked the greasy, tantalising aroma into her lungs while she searched out an over-ripe banana, muesli bar and bottled water.

With the unwrapped bar clenched between her teeth, she rifled her suitcase for something that didn't need an iron, pulling out denim shorts and a sleeveless orange top. A reviving shower in the amenities block—

Her mobile buzzed. She leaned over, grabbed the phone and said, 'Hello?' around a mouthful of dry oats.

'Good morning.'

'Uh.' Her bite went down the wrong way at the sound of that deep businesslike voice. She coughed, swallowed. 'Good morning.'

'Am I interrupting your breakfast?'

'Yes. No. I'm nearly done.'

'Have you changed your mind?'

'No. You?'

'No. I've drawn up an agreement. We'll both sign off on it first, then we need to go shopping.'

We? 'Ah…' Of course he wanted to come with her. He'd already made that clear; it was his money, his promotion. His say. But the thought of putting her body on display—in nothing more than a bathing suit—for Zak Forrester's perusal sent hot and cold shivers down her back.

'I told you, I'll cover the cost,' he said, hearing her hesitation.

'You're already letting me have the room rent-free.'

'Part of the deal,' he clipped. 'Where shall I pick you up?'

She almost smiled. He was doing his darnedest to find out where she was staying. Not as long as she could help it, he wasn't. 'I'll meet you. I need to drop my supplies off anyway.'

'The room's locked…it's probably easier to meet at my place—the agreement's here.' He sounded abrupt, as if he didn't want her anywhere near his home. 'Make it one hour. I've got to pick up my car from a friend's place first. We'll get the paperwork out of the way, then unload your gear before we hit the malls.'

He wasn't here. Abby knocked again. No answer. Presumably he was still collecting his car from wherever. She took the opportunity to wander to the rear of the property, absorbing the smell of salty air and the unaccustomed but welcome warmth of the sun on her bare legs.

Along one side she could see floor-to-ceiling windows plastered with yellowed newspaper. The veranda did indeed wrap around the entire house. At the back an old couch and a well-worn wicker rocking chair sat at one end, and there was a tiny table and two chairs beneath what must be the kitchen window—she could see a pot of yellowed parsley on the sill through the pane.

A man who cooked, but not often? She couldn't resist a closer look. Pressed up against the glass with her hands beside her eyes to shut out the light, she saw a surprisingly modernised kitchen. Buttercup-yellow walls, touches of green and terracotta. At the moment a day's worth of crockery was stacked in the sink and the kitchen table looked more like a workman's bench—

She wasn't alone.

The glide of sensation stroked up the length of her legs from ankle to knee to buttocks and she instinctively reached behind to tug the hem of her shorts as she swung around. Heat stung her cheeks for the second time in as many days. She caught at the strands of hair that fluttered across her vision in the breeze. 'Hi…Zak,' she said, as if she hadn't just been peeking uninvited in his window. Invading his privacy.

That was why his jaw must be so rigid, his lips a tight line. He stood at the base of the stairs beside a bush covered in purple flowers, his hands in the pockets of khaki trousers, eyes hidden behind a pair of wrap-around sunglasses. He wore a blindingly white snug-fitting polo shirt and casual shoes.

'Sorry to keep you waiting.' His voice was as tight as his expression. 'You'll see better from inside.' She didn't miss the note of sarcasm as he turned stiffly and began walking to the front of the house.

She didn't catch up with him until he was stabbing the key in the front door. This man's moods changed like the sea. He really needed to loosen up. 'I'm sorry…' She grazed his arm with her fingers, felt the tendons move beneath his bronzed skin, felt him flinch as he turned the key.

She'd always been a toucher and didn't see any reason to stop now. She'd just have to show some restraint with this guy. 'I shouldn't have snooped. It's just that I had such plans for my own little shop… Are you sure you haven't changed your mind…?'

'I haven't. And you were more than welcome to look around.' He seemed to make an effort to relax. Took off his sunglasses and made eye contact.

Wow. Ocean-blue today, and so deep, she wanted to sink in and lose herself in their mystery. Because that was what they were. Mysterious. Sultry one moment, cool the next… She wanted to find out what made the enigma called Zak Forrester. 'We're all set, then…'

'After you.'

She realised he was holding the door open for her. 'Thanks.' Her shoulder barely brushed against his chest, just enough to catch a degree or two of body heat and his freshly showered scent as she stepped into yesterday's mess.

'When this is finished it'll be the living room and family/entertaining area,' he said, scooping up a handful of potential hazards—loose nails on the floor—and popping them in a stack of miniature portable drawers. 'There's also an area that used to be an art studio with its own facilities at the back of the house, but that renovation's down the track a bit.'

Ah, the big windows she'd noticed earlier. 'What do you want to do with it eventually?'

'Haven't decided. Kitchen's this way.' He opened a nearby door and stepped into a hall, its floorboards gleaming but otherwise bare, skipping the two bedrooms and barely allowing her to glimpse more than a blur of colour as they passed. 'I'm just waiting on the deep freezer, but the room's functional.'

She nodded her approval. The kitchen had a sliding glass door that opened out onto the veranda with the table and chairs she'd seen earlier. 'You've made it a room where you can eat and relax.'

His facial muscles relaxed into a semblance of a smile and he picked up the kettle. 'I'm afraid I haven't had much time to relax here yet. Coffee? Or do you avoid caffeine?'

'Coffee'll be fine, thanks.'

While he hunted up a clean mug she explored, running her hand over the satin-smooth cupboards, admiring the terracotta containers precisely arranged against the splashboard, the fragrance of coffee as he spooned granules into the plunger.

She noticed a wedding invitation on the bench. 'Nick and Tina request the pleasure of the company of Zakary Forrester and Friend…' His godson's parents.

Hmm. Who was the lucky Friend? She shook her head. Now she was getting too personal; she didn't need to know.

Then her attention snagged on a pile of cookbooks stashed on a cupboard in a corner. 'You like to cook?' She wandered over and sifted through, pulling out one near the bottom. *Play Food for Lovers.*

A gift from a woman called Diane, she noted from the inscription dated some years ago at the front. Well, surprise, surprise. Zak Forrester had a playful side. She opened a page at random— Oh, my… A very playful side. And immediately wondered whether Zak often entertained. More specifically whether he cooked for two on a regular basis. What he liked to do after those dinners for two…

'Haven't had much time for it…' His eyes stalled on the open page, those long fingers tightening on the milk carton he'd taken from the fridge.

Then his gaze collided with hers, and suddenly the atmosphere in the kitchen, which had seemed light and airy a moment ago, plunged into thick and heavy and filled with a sexual tension that left Abby feeling pleasantly weak all over.

'Obviously you enjoy it when you do have the time.' She traced a fingertip over the erotic picture, smiling at Zak's visible discomfort, delighting in the way his eyes shifted from her to the window to the book, as if they couldn't find a place to settle.

A throat-clearing preceded his terse directive to, 'Take a look around the rest of the place if you want while the coffee brews, and I'll get the paperwork.'

'Sure.' She carefully stood the book upright on the counter-top so that its explicit cover faced Zak, a wasted effort since he was busy watching the kettle boil, and said, 'I look forward to sampling your cooking expertise sometime.'

Zak turned his back on the girl who'd just sent his emotions spinning from one out-of-control direction to another and faced the bench as he set the milk carton down, willing the beat of his pulse to subside, commanding his errant body to return to something approaching normal.

He waited, listening to her footsteps as she walked down the hall, and the tinkle of her anklet with its accompanying image of her sexy ankles faded.

Cool it. This wasn't supposed to happen. It wasn't *going* to happen. His fists tightened at his sides.

It already had.

He was as hard as the granite counter-top. Thank goodness Abby hadn't seen his body's response. He'd thought he'd got rid of that saucy book and its associated memories. 'It'll spice up our sex life,' Diane had told him on their third wedding anniversary.

Just watching Abby poring over the pictures had certainly spiced up his morning. And he could've sworn there was a hint of naughty in her voice when she'd mentioned sampling his cooking.

He snatched it up, slammed it shut. He was tempted to bin it, but that would be like admitting Abby had got to him. Instead, he stuffed it beneath his woodworking manual on the table.

Diane was dead. And the guilt he carried was the price he paid. Guilt, nightmares, regular recurring visions of what had happened and a decision to live the rest of his life alone.

Payment in full.

So this attraction—this damn *inexplicable* attraction— that had sprung to life the moment he'd met the woman claiming to be his tenant must be dealt with swiftly and harshly. He gazed out the window over the sink but he wasn't seeing the view. All he could see was Abby. Even if he was looking for a woman—for whatever reason— Abigail Seymour was all wrong for him. He didn't know if he trusted her. He didn't know if he even liked her.

And he had to take her shopping today. And it had to be today—he couldn't afford to wait until this crazy fever he felt whenever she came within cooee of him dissipated. Now he'd committed to using her as his model, the photo shoot needed to be dealt with regardless of his personal feelings.

So he had to breathe that exotic essence of whatever the hell it was that seemed to cling to his nostrils like a vine. He had to endure the sight of those endless legs in those short denim shorts…

'Hi there, I'm back, and impressed, Zak Forrester.'

Zak closed his eyes, pinched the bridge of his nose. When she said his name in that soft, breathy tone, Abby's voice did things to his body. Remembered, unwanted things. She didn't know the effect she had on him, which was a partial relief. 'Coffee's ready,' he said, grabbing a cloth and wiping spilled coffee grains off the bench. 'How do you take it?'

'White, no sugar. Thanks.'

'Me, too.' He glanced up and met her eyes. 'Now, if we can just agree on clothes.'

'Your money, your photos, your choice.'

He stirred in milk, feeling the tension ease a bit at the no-hassle arrangement. Simple. Brilliant.

CHAPTER FOUR

IT WAS neither simple, nor brilliant.

Why had he taken Abby's words so literally? He should've known no woman was immune when it came to shopping. It was a communicable disease peculiar to females.

In the end they compromised. He chose outfits he considered suitable and tried not to imagine how they'd look on her body. She tried them on for size in private. Then they came back with enough clothing and shoes and accessories on approval to fill the Surfer's Q1 seventy-five-storey apartment building. All on his credit card.

His suggestion that they take them to her hotel to choose was knocked back. She told him it was a mutual decision so they ended up killing two birds with one stone, dropping in at Capricorn Centre with Abby's shop supplies and the outfits to try on.

And the prospect of viewing them on the model loomed closer. Postponing the inevitable, he left Abby sorting clothes in one of the upstairs suites and set himself the task of hauling her cartons and boxes inside before heading into the office.

He found Tina kneeling on the floor, unpacking stationery supplies. She was wearing a pert yellow sundress, her hair a sleek cap of gold. 'Hey, Tina. I thought I told you not to bother coming in today?'

'Zak, hi.' She gave him a quick smile as she slit open a carton with her Stanley knife. 'You know Mum, she insisted on taking Danny, and, as much as I love him, I wanted the break.'

'Yesterday was a great day, Tina, and I'm honoured that you're entrusting me with the godfather role.'

'Hope you'll still feel that way when he's seventeen,' she said, swiping her blond bangs off her forehead with the back of her hand.

'You bet I will.' He leaned a hip on the edge of her desk and tried to imagine where he'd be in his life when Daniel reached those rebellious years. 'I was going to do it myself, but, since you're here, could you ring the photographer, please—name's on my desk—and schedule a time for tomorrow? Arrange for a hairdresser and we'll want a make-up artist on hand. I want those shots as soon as possible so we can upload them to the website. Oh, and organise for the pamphlet to go out as soon as we have the photos.'

'You've got yourself a model, then?' Tina paused with a handful of paper-clip boxes in her hand.

'Yeah…She's not exactly a model, she's more of a… massage therapist…' What did he really know about her except what she'd told him? 'She's going to be renting the empty room. It's a trial run, we'll see how it works out.'

'You don't look too thrilled about it. She giving you a hard time already?'

Ah, her choice of words. *You don't know the half of it.* 'We're still at the negotiation stage—at least we are with the outfits.'

'So what's she like?' Tina rose and began packing stuff in cupboards.

'Tall. Slim. Red hair…' His mind slipped back to last night's vision on the beach, the way her hair streamed behind her, the flash of her legs behind that gossamer skirt. So tall that if she wore heels that perfectly symmetrical mouth would line up against his and…

'Zak. You look…harassed. Is that the word I'm searching for?'

He met Tina's speculative gaze head-on and ran a hand through his hair. 'I've just been *shopping*—I think we cleaned out every mall in town—how do you expect me to look?'

'Okay, I get her visuals. That *is* the reason you selected her, I take it.' She arched her brows. 'But what's she *like* like?'

'Alternative. Vintage clothes.' Although today's shorts had been very modern and casual, he remembered. And short. 'Tinkly jewellery, into astrology and all that.'

'The kind who sprinkles herself with essence of moon drops?'

That's it. 'Yeah. Kind of.'

'And dances naked under the full moon, too, no doubt. So…not your type at all?'

'No,' he said, too quickly, he realised, and probably too forcefully as Tina's word images played through his mind.

'Known her long?'

'Only met her yesterday.'

'Ah.' Tina smiled. 'That explains the perfume I smelled on you at the christening.'

'She slipped—'

'And you came to her rescue. Okay. Tell Tina all.'

But as he explained Abby's problem—now a shared problem—and gave her a brief rundown Tina's expression sobered and a small frown creased her brow.

'Sounds a bit dodgy,' she said, and slid a comforting

hand over his. 'Be careful, Zacky. Innocent eyes and all that.'

An unwelcome thought slid through his mind. While he'd been unloading Abby's sealed boxes, which could be filled with rocks for all he knew, she could have done a flit with thousands of dollars' worth of merchandise.

No. He considered himself a good judge of character.

But his brain had been carpenter's glue since yesterday morning. He could no longer remember the flow of events or figure the logistics of how she might have planned to rob him blind, only that it was possible. It had taken Tina's objectivity to point that out.

'I'll be careful.' He removed his hand from beneath Tina's. 'Excuse me, I've some matters that need my attention.'

Who was that woman in the mirror? Abby studied the professional business image before her. Couldn't go wrong with a navy suit, white blouse and low-heeled navy shoes, she supposed. She pondered her next choice. Bathers, formal gown or negligee?

Zak had told her to choose her favourites from his selections. But how to choose from so many? And in the luxury suite he'd provided this was like a dream and she felt like a movie star.

She stripped down to her skin and picked up a white nightgown with an expensive label. It slid over her skin in a rippling waterfall of silk. 'What do you think, Zak?' she said, gazing at the suite's Pacific-sized bed, imagining him stretched out and naked, head propped on one elbow and watching her with lust in his eyes.

'How do you take a woman's clothes off?' she wondered. 'Do you prefer smooth and slow or fast and frantic?'

Or an erotic striptease? 'Maybe you're the rip and grab kind.' After all, he could afford a few torn garments.

She lay down on the bed, stretched out and stared at the speckled ceiling. 'Which are you, Zak?'

It had been a while since a man had made love with her. Her relationships had been short and not-so-sweet, the men in her life had never lived up to her ideal. She'd wanted so badly to be loved, she'd let the first guy to pay her any attention into her heart and her body.

But he hadn't been interested in her mind or her family history. All he'd wanted was sex as often as he could get it, and in her *naïveté* she'd mistaken that for passion.

She'd never been that trusting again.

But where Zak Forrester of the lake-blue eyes and charming crooked nose was concerned, she had a feeling she could easily forget.

Perhaps once Good Vibrations was up and running and she could afford a place to live, she wouldn't see him so often, wouldn't be tempted to think about him. To imagine all kinds of forbidden scenarios involving him and her and lots of bare, bronzed skin.

For goodness' sake. He had his own life and she'd be working and Aurora would need her to keep her company in the evenings. And it was the best feeling to be needed, wanted. She knew too well what it was like to be alone in foster families who didn't give a damn and were only in it for the money.

A sharp rap on the door had Abby bolting upright and scooting to the edge of the bed. She cast around for something to cover herself, but the knock cut through the room's silence with even more urgency.

'Hang on, I'm coming.' With only one hand in front to shield herself, she dragged the door open. 'Zak?' The lines around his mouth and eyes looked even deeper than usual, his looming stance blotted out the glow of light from the corridor. 'What's wrong?'

His fist was raised to hammer again, but he lowered it the instant he saw her. His eyes swept up her body like a forest fire, making her shiver in their heat, before coming to rest on her face. If you could call the blue-flamed intensity that singed her cheeks restful.

He didn't answer. His breathing was elevated, she noticed a few heart-pumping seconds later, as if he'd taken the stairs two at a time. But now he slowed his pace, aborting eye contact as he stepped inside and closed the door behind him.

'So what's the emergency?' she demanded, when she could speak again.

'I apologise, I shouldn't have overreacted,' he muttered. He walked past her and went to the window.

'Overreacted to what?'

Ignoring her repeated question, he made an all-encompassing gesture behind her. 'You should be very careful about opening doors dressed like that.'

'You made it sound critical. No one knows I'm here, who else would it be but you? And you said you needed to see the clothes on the model, so here I am.' She held her arms out to her sides. 'What do you think of the white?'

He didn't turn around. 'I *think* you need to consider wearing underwear if you're going to model the white.'

A glance in the mirror showed a hair-tumbled woman, her nipples clearly outlined against the fabric, the shadow between her thighs— 'Oh. I see what you mean.' No wonder he looked so uptight. 'I'm sorry. But you chose this garment, Zak, I'm merely the model. In my opinion wearing underwear, even that scrap of string and lace would make it look tacky. We'll have to go with something darker.' She grabbed up a handful of the nearest garments and backed away towards the bathroom. 'I'll try the red—'

Watching his profile, she saw him close his eyes and rub the bridge of his nose. 'Tell you what,' he said in a laboured voice, 'I'll trust your judgement. Be here tomorrow morning at eight o'clock. The photographer's coming at eight-thirty.'

'Fine,' she said. 'Whatever you want…' She saw his fingers clench on the back of the armchair against the window. 'I'll go change and be out of here before you know I've gone.'

But he wasn't waiting for her to leave. As he moved to the door he said, 'Take anything you want to try on and leave the rest here. We can use this room to set up in tomorrow morning.'

She watched him jerk the door open and nodded to his retreating back. 'See you tomorrow, then,' she said into empty air.

A short time later Abby pulled into her spot in the caravan park, her skin clammy, her mood decidedly lacklustre. Late afternoon thunderheads had gathered over the ocean, dark and ominous, but the air was warm and smelled of vegetation and bitumen.

The prospect of sitting in Scrappy for the evening if it rained wasn't good. The prospect of doing it night after night even grimmer. At least she had room in the back now to stretch out for some much-needed sleep.

She called Aurora first to check on her, cutting the call short because her battery was low, then picked up her grocery bag and climbed out of the van. She'd bought a packet of plain crackers, some salad vegetables that she could cut up in the kitchen amenities block and a tin of tuna.

'Now I know why you didn't want me to pick you up.'

She turned at the harsh accusation, clutching her groceries in one hand, shielding her eyes with the other as a final burst of sunshine pierced through the clouds. Zak stood at the back of the van, his face in shadow, one hand on Scrappy's rear windscreen.

A sense of betrayal knifed through her. 'What are you doing here?'

'I wanted to apologise. I was short with you back at the centre.'

'Yes, you were, but that's not it at all. You didn't come to apologise, Zak. You followed me.' She dumped her grocery bag on the car seat. 'You didn't trust me. You think I'm trying to rip you off somehow.' She saw a muscle clench in his jaw and knew she was correct in her assumption. 'I haven't figured *how* you think I'd do it, and maybe you haven't, either.' She shrugged, philosophical, and watched the ice-cream-cone clouds continue to build in the distance. 'I can't say I blame you.'

'I didn't—'

'Admit it, Zak.' She swung her gaze to his. 'If nothing else, I value honesty.'

Something flickered in his gaze, as if he'd suffered some form of deceit in his past. 'We're in total agreement on that point,' he said, stepping away from the van. 'I was *concerned*. Now I'm glad I was. How long were you planning on staying here?' He waved a disparaging hand at her surroundings. 'You don't even have power, for goodness' sake.'

'I thought maybe I could buy a tent—'

'Live in a *tent*? For how long?' He shook his head. 'Forget it, get back in your car.'

'What?'

'Just get in the damn thing. You're coming home with me.'

'To Capricorn? Your house?' She shook her head. 'Thank you for your offer, but it's obvious you don't want me there.'

His blue eyes darkened and for a heartbeat she thought she saw something else lurking in their depths, but then he lifted a shoulder and seemed to make a deliberate effort to remain calm. 'I have a spare room. At least you can boil a kettle, have a decent shower, make a meal.'

'No. I got myself into this, I'll—'

'You come back with me or our deal's off.' The bark was back in his voice.

'Hah. You need me for the photo shoot.' *And I need that rental space.*

He shovelled a hand through his hair. 'Just do it.'

'Not "just do it." Let's make this clear from the outset. I don't *do* charity. If I stay at your house, I work off the rent in some way: cleaning, cooking or painting walls. Whatever. At least until I start pulling in some income. In which case I'll be looking for my own place. She crossed her arms and met his eyes. '*Now* do we have a deal?'

He heaved a resigned sigh. 'We'll come to some arrangement.'

CHAPTER FIVE

ZAK didn't want her in his home—at his kitchen table, between his sheets, using his towels—but what choice did he have? He pulled into the driveway and watched her park behind him in the rear-vision mirror.

Watched her climb out of her van, all long limbs and red hair, and felt the jolt of sexual attraction down to his toes. How long was he going to have to endure a house guest? Especially one built like that.

He must be mad.

He had one bathroom—his bathroom. An *en suite*. Which meant she had to go through his room to use it. Right now the second bathroom's renovation assumed top priority unless he wanted to be forced to shower with the unwanted image of her soaped-up body behind his eyes, the scent of her soap in his nostrils for the next—how long?

Rolling his head back on the padded headrest, he blew out a long slow breath. He hadn't thought it through. He'd taken one look at her living conditions and known he couldn't walk away and pretend he hadn't seen her. It was minimal comfort that she hadn't looked any happier about the arrangement than he. With a shake of his head, he unfolded himself from his SUV and slid out.

She was already rolling a couple of trolley suitcases up the path. She'd left them in the van—another reason he'd had his doubts about her motives. Now he knew why— she'd planned to live out of a suitcase indefinitely. Sleep in a car for crying out loud.

And he knew he'd done the right thing—no, not right, not by a long shot. But he'd had a moral obligation to help her out and he'd done the only *decent* thing.

'I can manage a couple of rolling cases,' she told him when he would have helped.

He shrugged and unlocked the door. 'You know where the room is. I'll let you settle in. There are sheets and towels in the first cupboard. There's a second toilet off the studio but, I'm sorry, we'll have to share the bathroom for now.'

She stopped, momentary indecision etched on her face. 'Oh.'

I don't like the idea, either.

Then her face cleared and she smiled. 'We'll manage, somehow. I take quick showers.'

'If you're uncomfortable with the arrangement, I'll move into the spare room and you can have my bed.'

'No way,' she said quickly. 'But thank you.' She did the little shoulder thing and smiled again. 'Lucky you have a spare room or we'd really have a problem.'

He already did. 'You haven't eaten yet,' he said.

'No. But I've got some makings for salad and a can of fish. I'll just—'

'Okay, you make a salad and I'll throw a couple of steaks on the barbecue.'

They ate at the little table on the veranda while the rain came down in sheets, cooling the steamy air with its scent and mingling with the smoky aroma from the grill. Zak always ate out here, partly because the kitchen table was stacked with stuff, but mostly because he loved being out-doors.

As dusk closed in he lit mosquito candles and placed them on the railing and put one on the table. Purely functional, nothing more, but the soft glow lent mellowness to the atmosphere. 'More wine?'

'Thanks.'

He refilled her glass, then sat back and watched her looking out at the darkened backyard. He'd meant to excuse himself as soon as they'd finished eating to strip the wallpaper in the living room, but the wine's effect had him pushing back in his chair and postponing that moment a little longer.

He'd forgotten how much he'd enjoyed relaxing over a bottle of red at home after dinner with someone to talk to. Even if that someone wasn't a wise choice in dinner companions. Not if he wanted to sleep tonight. For now, though, it was enough to just chill out and appreciate the company.

'It's beautiful here,' Abby murmured. 'Back in Victoria we'd be inside huddled over our heaters.'

'I've lived in Queensland all my life, but I imagine an open fire would be cosy. Do you ever have one?'

'Not in ages.' She stared at one of the candles for a long while, her eyes turning dreamy and reflecting the glow. 'I remember…I was about four…Mum made a picnic for me and my baby sister one night in front of the fire. We toasted bread on a long fork.' Her eyes took on a deeper, misty, faraway quality. 'Thinking back now with the wisdom of age, I'm pretty sure it was because the electricity had been cut off.'

He leaned closer, his interest piqued. This was the first

time she'd volunteered any personal information. 'You live with family?' he asked.

'With my foster-mother.' A smile curved her lips. 'I was hoping to bring her up here to live. She had a stroke a while back and suffers with the cold. I thought a warmer climate would help. When I saw the ad for Capricorn, all I could think was here was our chance. I could work from home and care for her at the same time. Now I'm just hoping I can make a go of this business and bring her up here soon.'

'Who's caring for her now?'

'She's employed a live-in carer since I left.' Thoughtful, Abby leaned her arms on the table, her sensational cleavage shadowed in the candlelight. 'She can afford it, but I don't like leaving her in the care of strangers.'

'You didn't consider asking her to help with your business?'

Her head came up and her eyes flashed a defiant silver. 'I've always paid my own way. And I'm not about to tell her I've failed. Yet.'

As she talked her determination, the love and care she showed for her foster-mother, earned her his growing respect. 'You haven't failed, Abby. Not by a long shot.' And he'd do his darnedest to make sure that didn't happen. 'You said foster-mother?'

'Mum died when I was four. I never knew my father.'

'You mentioned a sister.'

'I haven't seen her since the night Mum died. We were separated when they put us in foster care.' She shook herself as if coming out of a sleep, straightened, ran a hand through her hair. 'And here I am telling you my life history. Sorry.' She pushed up. 'I'll just wash these dishes—'

'I've got them—'

They both reached for the salad bowl at the same time. A long hesitation as they stared at each other. Until Abby's voice washed over him. 'Zak?' She dipped her fingers into the bowl and looked down into his eyes. 'Pucker up.' And pressed something smooth and cool against his lips. 'Can't waste a perfectly good cherry tomato.'

His lips seemed to part of their own accord, her fingers grazing his mouth as she pushed the delicious little morsel inside. He barely tasted it—it rolled around his mouth, then he chewed and swallowed. Hard.

She laughed, her eyes sparkling in the candlelight. 'You look positively stricken. Did you think I was going to…?' That teasing expression in her eyes remained, but her mouth softened, parted just the tiniest bit as she leaned closer. Enough for him to see the tip of her tongue touch her lower lip.

Enough for him to wonder how it would feel against his. How she'd taste…

He wasn't aware of meeting her halfway, he wasn't aware of moving at all, of tilting his head back or lifting his hand to touch her petal smooth cheek, but then she was kissing him.

And he was kissing her back.

Rubbing his lips against hers, absorbing her sweet frivolity. Mating his tongue to hers and savouring the warmth. Reaching behind her neck to pull her closer.

He felt her hands move over his shoulders, her thumbs drawing tight circles below his collarbones.

His own thumb stroked back and forth across her nape, to her neck where her pulse fluttered. Smooth, incredibly smooth.

Stupid. Incredibly stupid.

He reared back, away from the temptation of her lush

mouth. The rain drummed on the roof, or was it the blood pounding in his ears? No, he was sure his blood was nowhere near his ears; it had pooled lower down and was beating like a jackhammer. He grabbed her hands, pushed them away and rose in one jerky movement.

They stared at each other for a taut, charged moment.

'Hey, it was a simple kiss…' She blinked, the soft dreamy light in her eyes dissipating, and he felt like all kinds of an idiot.

'You were the one who turned it into not-so-simple,' she pointed out. 'You really need to lighten up. I'm a physical person—it's part and parcel of my job. Don't take it so personally.'

'Fine.' His skin heated and tightened at the thought of getting physical some more with his house guest. Hard *not* to take it personally with his lips still throbbing with her taste. He turned away and began stacking plates. 'I'll finish up here. You go ahead and use the bathroom before I turn in.'

'Okay.' But she stopped at the kitchen door. 'But I'll say it again now. We share chores.'

'Agreed.'

'And, Zak. About that kiss? If it makes you feel better, forget it happened.'

The instant she'd gone he plunked down onto his chair again. *Forget it?* He blew out a long harried breath. Not flaming likely. But he thought back to the conversation they'd been having *before* the kiss. And he had to admit she wasn't quite the flaky, irresponsible woman he'd thought.

It didn't make her any less dangerous.

Zak knew he was drowning…

Black salty water rushing into his mouth, choking off

his air. Down. Desperate fingers plucking, searching. Find Diane!

Feel her hand through the car window. Explosions of light in front of his eyes. Sound. The low slow beat of thunder. The bottom of the world. Eardrums bursting. Lungs burning. Diane! Fingers slipping away. Alone in the dark. Midnight.

Peace. Floating. Accepting. White light.

Screams. Cold. Diane! No!

He struggled through the miasma of dreams and memories and into a semi-reality. Not his wife's golden hair and honey eyes. An auburn-haired silver-eyed woman floated before him.

Jackknifing upright, his body clammy and shivering, he listened to the pounding of his heart, willing it to slow, willing the tantalising image away.

'Just a dream,' he told himself into the darkness, and slid back onto the pillows, wide-awake now. He had no control over his subconscious, but he'd damn well control his waking hours.

Despite her lack of sleep over the past few nights with the travelling and last night's dismal effort in her van, Abby was awake at dawn. Her sleepy gaze took in the freshly painted room with its cool blue walls, the deeper blue summer quilt and white shabby-chic furniture. Not a bad effort for a guy.

And that guy made her…hot. In places he shouldn't. Such as when he'd looked at her in that negligee…and last night when she'd kissed him, *and* he'd kissed her back. When his fingers had stroked her skin and set her nerve endings sizzling.

Before he'd realised what he was doing and pulled away.

But he'd shown her more kindness than anyone ever had, apart from Rory and Bill. She owed him. She was going to pay him back the best way she knew how. By releasing those inner tensions that were, for whatever reason, holding him back from enjoying life. Even if she had to fight him every step of the way.

'Good morning.' Abby stood on the back veranda with two mugs of blackberry tea spiked with cider vinegar and honey. The rain had long gone, leaving only the smell of damp vegetation. Sometime in the night Zak had dragged his pillow and a sheet outside to the couch.

At the moment he was flat on his back, his morning stubble wildly attractive and making Abby wish she could lean closer and run her fingers over it. Instead, she sat on the rocking chair.

He muttered something and rolled onto his side, dragging a corner of the sheet with him. Too late, she realised he didn't sleep in pyjamas. Only a pair of red boxer shorts, which were currently riding low on his belly, exposing an arrow of dark hair that pointed the way to—

Out of bounds.

'Zak, good morning,' she said again, taking a sip from her mug.

His eyes flickered and she caught a glimpse of vulnerability in their sleepy depths. 'Abby,' he mumbled, his voice thick. Then he blinked twice as he registered her presence, the haze in his blue eyes sharpening. 'Something wrong?'

'No. Are you ready for a walk?'

His eyes slid shut. 'Something's very wrong. A walk. At this time of day. Or should I say night?'

'This is the *best* time of day. The grass looks like

emeralds, the air's as fresh as a song out here, and it's calling our names.'

'Maybe yours. I don't hear mine.' Eyes still closed, he rubbed his chest. 'Why can I smell blackberries?'

'I made tea for us. I find it's a good way to start the day with something warm and herbal.'

Although, with the unfamiliar scent of musky male in her nostrils, she could think of a warmer and more invigorating way than a tea tonic and a walk on the beach...

He muttered something short and terse and undoubtedly rude into his pillow.

'You didn't sleep well,' she told him. 'It might help.'

'Hmph.'

'Okay.' She set a mug on the veranda beside the couch. 'I'll let you get acquainted with the morning.'

Aborting her beach-walk plans, she grabbed a mat from the veranda, walked a short distance down the garden path and set it on a patch of damp grass and sat down facing him.

She wasn't letting Zak off the hook so easily. If she could just get him to take some time out, look at the world around him instead of working twenty-four-seven. She already had him pegged. If it wasn't the centre, it was his house, and he had a construction business chugging along somewhere. Something had turned him into a workaholic.

She reached for the sea-green crystal at her neck, closed her eyes and let her thoughts dissolve like clouds in a summer sky. Let impressions and sensations surround her as the morning sun caressed her eyelids with golden warmth.

Until languid turned to heat and tranquil turned to edginess, prickling her skin with goose bumps.

She opened her eyes and saw Zak glaring at her from the veranda, and every peaceful cell in her body jumped to attention. She hadn't heard him rise and change but he was wearing those itty-bitty shorts that showed off the long, powerful musculature of his legs and a navy T-shirt with the sleeves ripped out, baring equally impressive bulges.

She let herself indulge in the sight of that athletic body. To imagine gliding oil-slick palms over those strong lines. Her hands itched and a bolt of energy powered through her veins.

As she watched him step off the veranda, his eyes on her with single-minded purpose, she wondered if she'd made the right decision in waking him up. Perhaps she should have left him to his dreams. Or his demons, she thought, remembering the haunted look she'd seen in his eyes as he woke.

Then he stopped in front of her and she was glad she hadn't. Looking at Zak with the sun behind him like some sort of halo won hands down over any visualisation she could come up with.

She sifted her hands through the cool grass. 'Hi.'

'What happened to your walk?' Even with his face in shadow, she could see his frown.

'I changed my mind. I decided to meditate here and wait for you to wake up.'

'Aah, meditation.' He let the word slide out slowly between his lips. 'That mystical Eastern pastime.'

'There's nothing mystical about it. Just close your eyes and open your mind, listen to what the universe is telling you. Visualise.'

Except all she could visualise right now when she closed her eyes was Zak lying down beside her. The sun warming his skin to honey-brown as he dragged her against him. The grass's coolness a sharp contrast to the heat of his body on her. In her. She pressed her legs tighter together to ease the tingling. *Try harder.*

He sat down, out of arm's reach, obviously prepared to humour her. 'So what's the universe telling you today?'

'To focus on Good Vibrations and not let distractions get in the way.' *Like you.*

'Ever get mixed signals? Like someone else's messages instead of yours?' He tugged out a blade of grass, threaded it between his fingers.

'Sceptic,' she accused. 'Now you…' She shuffled the metre or so between them on her backside. 'You need to let go of a truckload of baggage.' And recognised his denial. The rolled eyes, the tensed jaw. 'Hey, it'll come— My guess is you're facing difficulties in your life right now.' And for whatever reason, he didn't feel inclined to share them with her.

He looked away, the sun's rays striking off the blue irises, then turned to her. The heat she saw there seared her own eyeballs. *Yeah, difficulties—you're sleeping in my spare room.* If he'd said it aloud, he couldn't have been clearer. He shook his head, looked away again. 'I'm fine.'

'If you say so.' She reached out to soothe his cheek. The pads of her fingers skimmed over the rough texture, sending instant sensation fizzing through her veins.

Before he could flinch or do his pulling-away trick, she dropped her hand, curled her fist around the tingles. 'If my being in your home is going to make your life more difficult, I'll leave. I'm paid up at the caravan park for a week.'

'No. You're staying until you're in a position to find other accommodation *as we agreed*; end of discussion.'

His words, clipped and hard and remote, chased away the warm fuzzies she'd been harbouring since she'd touched his face. 'Okay.'

'Okay.' He underscored her acquiescence, then pushed up without looking at her. 'Breakfast in ten minutes if we're going to make our appointment.'

CHAPTER SIX

ZAK leaned against the conference room's wall and watched the photographer snap a series of pictures, scowling as Carlo's long arty fingers skimmed Abby's neck while he adjusted her blouse, tilted her chin so that she was looking directly into the other man's eyes.

Carlo moved behind the camera. 'A little to the right, honey, and looking at the camera... Perfect.'

Zak's sentiments exactly. Abby's hair was caught in a neat upswept style that exposed her creamy neck, and her earlobes glinted with tiny gold hoops. In the navy suit and crisp white blouse, she looked the epitome of a successful businesswoman.

He mentally nodded his satisfaction with the image that would appear on his website, but his frown remained. A *smiling* businesswoman who looked as if she was enjoying the flirtation coming her way during office hours, and a little too much.

The fact that the man was obviously gay didn't soften Zak's mood any. Especially when Carlo murmured something to Abby that no one else heard and they both shared a laugh, heads almost touching. What was it that women found attractive about gay men?

And it was all going downhill from there.

Jorge, the male model Zak had chosen from the agency's files last week, was the kind of suave, good-looking blond with an ego as big as his chest measurement. The kind of guy women fell for, which, he reminded himself, was why he'd chosen him.

Before he'd met Abby.

Irritated with himself, he pushed off the wall. This was crazy, and not what this morning was all about. This morning's shoot was his opportunity to sell the centre to tourists and conference-goers, nothing more.

'Let's move on to the pool, shall we?' Carlo flapped a hand at the camera crew. 'Abby, darling, the black one-piece.'

Zak watched Abby make her way towards the door that led from the conference room. On a sudden impulse, he followed.

She caught sight of him in the mirrored lobby and turned on the staircase, her brows raised. 'Something wrong?'

He walked right up to her. Imagined burrowing into that sexy curve of neck to breathe in her alluring feminine scent. 'I just wanted to check that you're okay with this. I know you weren't enthusiastic with the idea.'

Her face relaxed, and the smile she gave him was pure sunshine. 'I'm fine.'

She lay her fingers on his arm, a habit of hers, he was beginning to realise, and not one she restricted to him. He'd seen her touch Carlo and Macho Man the same way.

'In fact, I'm kind of enjoying it,' she said with her little shoulder lift. 'It's fun, like playing at being someone else.'

Didn't she like being herself? he wondered. Was she unhappy with who she was? Then he remembered she'd come from a foster-home background, something he had no knowledge or understanding of. Her biological mother was dead; she had no knowledge of her sister's whereabouts.

'Was there anything else?' she asked, already on the third stair.

'Ah…you don't need help with anything, then?' He hadn't meant it the way it sounded, particularly as his gaze had been skimming over the curve of her bottom as he spoke. He struggled to block the image of slipping her jacket off for her and undoing the row of little white buttons down the front of her blouse…

She glanced back over her shoulder. 'I think I can find my own way into a bathing suit.'

Just as well, he thought as he walked away.

An hour later with the pool shoot out of the way, thank goodness—because watching Abby's wet body snuggled up to Jorge's had Zak's teeth on edge—they moved to the dining area to shoot the wine-and-dine scenes.

When Abby entered the room fifteen minutes later, Zak suddenly found it difficult to breathe. She wasn't wearing the red number he'd chosen, but an emerald-green dress that had caught her eye. It complemented her auburn hair, which was pinned up with a green comb.

But it was the tempting deep V zip that could slide all the way to her navel if she chose that had his attention. As she turned the hem teased the backs of her knees and the dip at the back had his hand itching to touch, to see if her skin was as smooth as it looked.

And the way her feet arched over those strappy gold sandals— He had a sudden vision of those stiletto-clad feet arched over his shoulders as she writhed in passion—

'Darling! You look stunning.' Carlo blew an air kiss in the flamboyant way he did everything and shook back the long hair that had dipped over his brow. 'And that colour is *so* you. Now, come and sit.'

Zak ran a tongue around dry lips as she seated herself at the little table. At least her legs were safely hidden behind the tablecloth.

Carlo fussed with the table setting and waved a hand. 'Curtains closed, please. And someone light the candle. Jorge, offer her the rose…'

The session continued before his eyes, but Zak's mind wandered. He could imagine taking her to dinner at some up-market restaurant. Something outdoors or on top of a building overlooking the ocean where he could watch the evening breezes play with that delicate hairstyle, until it tumbled over her shoulders in an auburn tangle beneath his hand. Or where he could watch the moonlight reflect the silver in her eyes.

He wouldn't go with a rose. No, he'd give her a sunflower. He didn't know what yellow might mean in her colour-conscious mind, but for him, now, watching her, he'd say it symbolised light. Openness. Yes, honesty.

But her lifestyle, her personality, was at odds with his—the woman seemed to bend with the wind, whereas he liked things where he could see them, put his hands on them and understand them. She had a foster-mother, he came from a big family. Loving parents and three siblings; scattered all over the country, but when they got together it was as if they'd never been apart.

'…to the suite upstairs.'

Zak realised Abby had already gone to change for the romantic bedtime scene. He watched the camera crew, Carlo and Jorge head down the corridor, the flurry of noise and activity recede. And knew he couldn't do it. He couldn't watch Abby recline on that bed in nothing but a negligee, no matter how innocent or tastefully done.

The thought alone was enough to have the blood pumping fast and heavy through his veins. A restless primitive beat that he had no right to feel. Didn't *want* to feel.

No. Paperwork awaited his attention. Attention that he'd neglected over the past couple of days. He'd be better served to get it out of the way. Carlo had everything under control. He'd see the shots when he approved them before uploading them to the website.

While Abby slipped out of the cappuccino-coloured negligee and redressed in her own skirt and top, she wondered where Zak had been during the final photo shoot.

At the vanity she reached for cleanser and removed the unfamiliar heavy make-up she'd felt uncomfortable with all morning and reapplied her own moisturiser and a light lipstick. He'd been as distracted as she. His eyes, when they'd met hers, had wiped whatever she'd been thinking clean out of her mind. It had been all she could do to stay focused on Carlo's instructions.

First off she was going to track him down; she had no doubt he was still here somewhere. She'd tell him she'd finished the shoot, then she'd see if the shelves had arrived and do some setting up in the shop. Then she'd walk home—it was only a short distance—and familiarise herself with his place. Maybe do a bit of cleaning and prepare something for tea.

He'd given her a key. The strange feeling she'd had when he'd detached it from a ring in his kitchen drawer and met her eyes with a gaze that blew hot and cold rippled through her again. A look that said having a key to his house would be like living together and way too intimate. But necessary.

The sounds of a fussy baby reached her ears as she

knocked at the open door to a spacious office. A harassed-looking blonde was trying to juggle an infant in one arm and a pile of folders in the other.

'Hi. Sorry to bother you. I was looking for Zak.'

'Next office down.' She flashed a brief smile. 'I'm Tina, by the way.'

'Hi, Tina. So this must be Daniel. Zak told me about the christening. I'm Abby Seymour. I just took the vacant shop.'

'Ah-h-h.' Tina's smile cooled a few degrees. She dumped the files on her desk and switched the wriggling child to her other arm. 'The massage therapist. You turned up out of the blue and into the right place at the right time, didn't you?'

'I did.' Abby bit back the surprise and hurt at Tina's less than cordial welcome. 'And Zak's been more than kind.'

Tina's brown eyes pinned Abby's with a slow I've-got-your-measure perusal. 'Zak's a kind sort of a guy. The sort of guy people might try to take advantage of.'

'Zak strikes me as being far too astute to allow that to happen,' Abby countered.

At that moment Daniel rocked and squirmed, knocking the files Tina had placed on the desk to the floor.

'I've got them.' Abby picked up the paperwork. 'Looks like you've got your hands full.'

'The baby-sitter cancelled at the last minute.' Tina's harried exhalation blew at her bangs as Daniel began wailing. 'I promised I'd have this mess sorted by the end of the day.'

'Let me take him a moment,' Abby offered, tapping her hands gently in Danny's face. 'I love babies, especially ones as cute as this.' Danny quieted, stilled, eyeing Abby with fascination. 'What is he—seven months?'

'Eight.'

'He's probably teething.' Abby stroked the red splotch on his cheek. 'Poor baby. Come to Abby?'

'I'm… Yes, he is.' Tina hesitated, then handed him over somewhat reluctantly. 'Just for a moment, then, while I re-sort this mess.'

Abby set the child on her hip, offering him the teething ring pinned to his bib, but he was more interested in her hair. 'I could take him for a stroll around the centre, give you a break.'

'No.' Tina stopped midway to the filing cabinet. Then nodded, and her swift refusal was tempered with a softer, 'He's not used to strangers.'

'We'll just go to Zak's office,' Abby assured her. 'See if he's there and be right back. How does that sound, Danny? Want to see Uncle Zak?'

'Well, that's a first,' Tina remarked thoughtfully. 'I've never seen him go to someone he doesn't know so readily.' She nodded. 'O-kay. He's right next door.'

Abby found Zak's door open but the man himself was nowhere to be seen. His computer's screensaver scrolled through tropical images. A full mug of coffee steamed be-side the mouse, his reading glasses lay on a folder. So he hadn't gone far and intended returning.

Or maybe not, if he'd heard her talking to Tina. 'What do you think? Is he trying to avoid me?' she asked Danny. Her heart melted when Danny tugged at a strand of her hair and responded with a salivary grin that showed off three stubby teeth.

With Tina's maternal concern in mind, she returned to her office. 'Here we are, all safe and sound.'

Some of the tension eased out of Tina's face and the hint of a smile tipped a corner of her mouth. 'Thanks.'

'No problem.' Abby pulled out her mobile with her free hand, thumbed in Zak's number.

'Forrester.'

'Good afternoon to you, too,' she replied sweetly, smiling at Danny. 'With a bark like that, should I be afraid of your bite?'

In the ensuing silence the ether hummed with all kinds of erotic possibilities; she could almost see him closing his eyes and rubbing the bridge of his nose as he was wont to do when he was harassed.

'Very afraid,' he said finally. 'What can I do for you, Abby?'

'You didn't view the final shots.'

'I've been tied up with the electrician.'

'Sounds kinky.' She glanced at Tina who was hunkered at the bottom drawer of her filing cabinet, ears flapping. 'Is that why there's a hot coffee on your desk going cold?'

Another silence, then a resigned, 'You've got me there.'

She had to smile. 'And *I've* got a little boy *here* who thinks his godfather works too much and needs a break. Right, Tina?' she said, and saw her nod in agreement. 'Perhaps you'd like to help his busy mother out and take me and Danny off her hands for a while—that is, if you're in the vicinity…?'

She disconnected, cast a conspiratorial grin at Tina. 'He'll be along.'

'That'd be great. For me *and* for Zak. Thank you.'

'No problem.'

'Be assured I'll be one of your first customers,' Tina told Abby as Zak relieved her of his hefty godson five minutes later. 'My back could do with some pampering.'

'The first session's on me,' she said, pleased to have won over Tina at least.

Now, if she could just get Zak to trust her… Her gaze swung to the man in question, juggling the child against his white business shirt as if the little guy belonged there.

And something inside her went ping. If ever there was a picture that warmed her heart it was a man prepared to let himself be strangled by his own expensive silk tie with the saliva-wet fingers of an eight-month-old...

'Daniel and I need fresh air and ice cream,' she told him, and cleared a sudden lump from her throat. 'A little ice cream's okay, isn't it, Tina?' Her eyes were still locked on the domestic sight before her.

'He loves it,' she heard Tina say.

'So let's go.' Abby slipped a hand in the crook of Zak's elbow and tugged him towards the door.

Zak felt as if he were skating on thin ice and wondered how he'd got himself into this unsettling situation: a baby and a woman on his arm, neither of whom belonged to him.

'Let's try that place on the corner with the yellow beach umbrellas,' Abby suggested as they exited into the afternoon sunshine.

He nodded, wishing the sensation of Abby's arm in his didn't feel so damn good. He couldn't shrug her off—by her own admission she was a physical person—she didn't mean anything by it.

They must look like any other family out for a stroll. It was the oddest feeling and one not to be probed too deeply because the wounds still bled. His wife was dead, pronounced guilty by him before she could prove her innocence. By his own actions he'd cheated himself of fatherhood.

He was never committing to a woman again, which meant no kids. Ever. His choice, he reminded himself, but the knowledge wrenched soul-deep.

'Stop. Right. Here.' Abby swung in front of him. 'You were supposed to leave your problems at the office. For the next thirty minutes it's time out. Agreed?'

He looked at her eyes, pleading and demanding at the same time, and felt his resolve slip a notch. He was quickly discovering it was her nature to care about others. And this afternoon wasn't about him. She was giving Tina a break, the least he could do was support her… He tried a grin, and found it easier than he'd thought. 'I'm thinking a triple chocolate-chip sundae.'

Her smile was pure summer. 'Vanilla for me. Your shout.'

They found a table outside beneath one of those umbrellas. Abby relieved him of Daniel, setting him on her lap, playing pat-a-cake and cooing maternally as if she was born to the role.

When their order came, she fed Daniel tiny spoonfuls of her vanilla scoop, gently rubbing the cold along his gums, letting his sticky fingers play with her hair, seemingly unconcerned that he was staining her top. The antithesis of Diane, who had hated mess and avoided babies. He found the change refreshing. Endearing. Was he falling for this woman? He shook the thought away and concentrated on his sundae.

Daniel nodded off against her breast. It made Zak wonder how it would feel to rest his own head on that gentle slope and twine those auburn curls around his hand. Watching Abby eat ice cream was almost a more sensuous experience than the treat itself. The way she slid the spoon between her lips, almost closing her eyes in bliss with each mouthful.

'You're an ice-cream junkie,' he said.

'I prefer *devotee*.' Her tongue darted out to lick her lips and she grinned. 'How can you tell?'

'I recognise the symptoms. Or, if you prefer, the traits. I must admit to being guilty of the same myself.'

'One of life's more pleasurable indulgences.' Smiling, she scooped up a parfait-size spoonful, held it to his mouth. 'Swap you.'

He took the spoon between his lips—the spoon straight from her mouth—watching awareness sharpen her eyes as they locked gazes.

'My turn,' she said.

Scant millimetres from her lips, Daniel woke from his brief hiatus, decided he wanted in on the action and batted the spoon Zak was holding out with a fist, toppling the confection onto the front of Abby's neck.

'Here.' Grabbing a paper napkin, he swabbed the chocolate smear. *I could lick it off.* He immediately pulled away, offered Abby the napkin. 'Stick to vanilla, mate,' he told Daniel, glad to have somewhere else to focus his gaze. 'It's colourless. More or less. Sorry, Abby, your top's a mess.'

'It'll wash,' she said. She didn't seem bothered. 'We'd better be going—someone needs a nappy change.'

Five minutes later Zak handed Daniel over to his grateful mum, then walked Abby to the lobby. 'Thanks. Tina appreciates it, and so do I.' He glanced at the stained top—but not too closely. 'Sorry about the mess.'

'It doesn't matter. I had fun.' She smiled that summer smile but didn't touch him.

He felt oddly disappointed. 'So did I,' he said. And realised he meant it.

'I'll see you at home, then.'

Her casual words, the farewell flip of her hand— He felt his muscles tense. Something only a wife or lover would say.

'I'll be late,' he said around the cramp in his gut. He turned abruptly and hurried to the sanctuary of his office.

'Where are you, Zak?' *And what business is it of yours, Abby?* She covered the bowl of dinner she'd put aside for him and slid it in the fridge. Just because she had a room here didn't give her the right to question where he was. He'd said he'd be late, but she hadn't thought he meant *this* late.

She'd cleaned what she could of the kitchen, attempted to sort the mess on the table, then, using what ingredients were to hand, she'd cooked up a batch of chilli con carne and prepared a tossed salad. It was now eleven o'clock. Time to go to bed and *not* think about where he was.

She slipped into her sleep shirt, lay down and stared at the night sky through the open window. This afternoon he'd been so approachable, so smiley, she'd glimpsed another side of him.

Until she'd ruined it when she'd said she'd see him at home. Too intimate. Too fast. Something had happened to him in his past. A woman; she'd bet on it.

Zak set a fast pace along the beach. White fingers of surf curled against the indigo sea, stretching out into the distance along the coastline. Since Diane had died, he often walked here nights to take in the changing moods of the sea and seek the absolution he craved, but tonight he barely noticed the way the moonlight rippled on the water, the ceaseless soughing of the waves on the shore.

Abby had somehow got under his skin; she knew how to make him itch and he had no idea how to relieve it. *Yes. You do,* an inner voice said. Shaking his head, he began jogging, trying to erase the images of a mermaid-like creature who'd danced on this sand a couple of evenings ago.

His bare feet welcomed the cold as the incoming tide washed over his ankles. He was almost tempted to strip off his too-tight trousers and cool his entire body's restless heat in the sea.

But to do that would mean facing his demons and letting the water do its work. His pulse spiked and his heart clenched at the thought. He could almost feel it strangling him, the burst of pain in his ears as he plunged after the doomed car and sank, his instinctive action consigning him to a watery death.

Fighting off the panic that always accompanied the images and clawed without mercy up his throat, he veered from the water's edge towards the softer sand dunes. Dragged in salty air. *Breathe, two, three*. He was alive.

Alive and alone.

And horny as hell.

He pushed on, feeling the sweat trickle over his brow and down his back. He'd never considered himself a man who avoided uncomfortable situations, but he was doing a damn good job of it tonight. The glow of his guest bedroom's light and knowing Abby was there had been enough to slam his car in Reverse and speed back down the road and away from temptation.

But he didn't want her to feel she was intruding or not welcome. She'd lived with foster-families, for heaven's sake. He wanted her to feel his place was relaxed enough that she could call it 'home.' For the time she'd be there.

Except it wasn't a home, was it? A home, by Zak's definition, included laughter, kids, pets. Love. It meant sharing—not simply taking turns in the bathroom and dividing chores. It was opening yourself up to another person, taking the good times with the bad.

He stopped, hands on his knees, to catch his breath and his runaway thoughts. Was he confusing a home with love? Or did the two go hand in hand?

Either way, it wasn't going to happen. Not again.

CHAPTER SEVEN

NEARLY midnight. Abby would be asleep now. Zak breathed a sigh of relief as he parked and looked up at the darkened windows. This was what he wanted, right? To come home to some semblance of solitude?

But she'd left the front porch light on. A 'welcome home' sign.

The fact that she'd thought of it niggled at him as he unlocked the back door and quietly let himself inside. A spicy aroma hung in the air. He followed it to the kitchen, switched on the light and stopped in surprise—the neat-as-a-pin kitchen.

Further inspection revealed the source of the aroma in the fridge. She'd also cooked for him. Bought a bottle of pink champagne, he noted, even though she couldn't afford it. He glanced at the outdoor table and now he noticed the cutlery setting and wineglass reflected in the kitchen's light. She'd probably waited to eat with him, too.

Guilt twitched between his shoulder blades. He'd paid her consideration back by avoiding her. Being the perceptive woman she was, he had little doubt she'd recognise it, making him feel twice the idiot he was.

He reached for a beer as he shut the fridge. Twisted the

top off and chugged half the liquid down. They were going to have to set some ground rules. Simple gestures like the security light were fine. Probably. Maybe. Anything that smacked remotely of a couple—wine, dual table settings—was not.

He yanked out a chair and sat, scowling at his beer bottle as he twisted it round and round in his hands. Who said she'd been thinking 'couple'? Probably cooked for herself and had leftovers. Ditto the wine. It was *him* thinking 'couple'. Imagining 'couple'.

Abby stood at the kitchen door, pushed the hair from her face as she watched Zak frowning at his bottle. His absolute aloneness tugged at her. 'I didn't know you were home.' His head whipped around, then back to his bottle, and she watched his jaw bunch as she padded further into the room. The new slate tiles felt cold beneath her feet, a stark contrast to the heat blossoming in her cheeks. She knew she looked sleep-mussed. Knew he'd noticed. 'Or can't you sleep?' she asked.

He slid another long look her way, then took a pull at the bottle he was torturing. 'Haven't tried.'

Her heart did a flip as she visualised placing her masseuse's hands on the tense set of his shoulders. Oh, he'd feel good. Hard and warm. She'd slide her fingers up his neck, into his hair, feel its texture, breathe its scent while her fingertips massaged circles over his scalp and absorbed the day's stresses. 'It's been a long day for you.'

'It's not over yet.'

His eyes met hers, deep pools of promise, and her heart did another of those amazing, unsettling flips, but she blinked and those pools could have been made of glacier ice.

'I've still got some work to do.'

'Surely you could take a break? It's late.'

'I promised myself I'd work at least an hour a day on the house, no matter what.' He tilted his bottle in the direction of the living room. 'And we need somewhere to relax other than the kitchen.'

Or the bedroom. She could feel his rejection, his discomfort from halfway across the room. If she'd tried to act out her massage fantasy, he'd have resisted. The man was an island.

'You made dinner,' he said gruffly. 'I grabbed a burger, I should've let you know. Perhaps it'd be easier if you just cooked for yourself.'

She started to agree, then stopped. No, she wasn't letting him off that easily. 'It *is* easy, Zak,' she said, meeting his eyes. 'All it takes is a phone call.'

She walked back to her bedroom, closed the door. And made a decision. She stripped off her sleep shirt. If he was going to be an idiot and work till he dropped, she was going to be there to catch him.

He was squatting in the middle of the living room mixing paint when she strolled in two minutes later, in shorts and T-shirt chewing on an apple.

His eyes flared when he saw her and his hand stopped mid-stir. 'What are you doing?'

'I'm here to help. Want a bite?'

Ignoring the proffered apple, he shook his head, resumed stirring. 'Go back to bed, Abby.'

She stood over him, chewed a few moments, watching the way the muscles in his forearm moved. The way his T-shirt stretched taut over his back and didn't quite meet the dip in the centre of his shorts, leaving a tantalising wedge of skin…

'Aren't you going to strip first? The rest of the wallpaper,' she added, indicating with her apple when his eyes flickered up at her beneath lowered brows.

'Yes.'

'So why are you mixing the paint?'

He closed his eyes briefly. 'I want to try a patch to make sure the colour's right.' Carefully placing the rod he'd been stirring with on newspaper, he stood, the can of paint in his hand. 'Why can't you do as I ask and go to bed?'

'I'm obstinate, too, when necessary. Let me give you a hand stripping. Just tell me how.'

She hadn't meant it the way it sounded. Really, she hadn't. Until the can he was holding tilted as he stared at her, dribbling paint over his hand.

'I meant…the wall—'

'I know what you—' He tripped on the rod, splattering paint on his feet. 'Damnation!'

She bit her lip. 'Oops.'

He set the paint on the floor. Rubbed a paint-smeared finger between his brows. 'Okay. I'll finish the wallpaper; it needs the ladder. You paint.'

While he hunted up rags to deal with the mess and studiously avoided looking anywhere near her, she found a brush and got started.

They worked in silence for a few minutes, until Abby said, 'Are you going to use a darker shade for the window frames?'

He paused to look at her paint pot, blew out a breath. 'That *is* the shade for the window frames.' He descended the ladder as he said, 'It's a smaller can, see? The paint for the walls is the other one. And you use a roller on the wall, not a brush.'

'Oh.' She shrugged, dipped her brush in the can. 'If you'd

taken a look around instead of focusing on what's in front of your nose and nothing else, you might have noticed.'

'I think… What are you doing?'

'It's called having fun, Zak.' She finished painting her name in large curly letters on the wall, then painted her palm ready for the final touch.

And changed her mind as she felt the heat of a solid masculine presence right behind her. Instead, she turned, planting her hand in the centre of his chest and smiled up at his incredulous expression.

No response. Nothing but silence in the sultry evening air that seemed to have engulfed them. Impossible to tell whether he was angry or amused in the depths of those smoke-dark eyes.

Her smile widened. 'Guess I owe you a T-shirt.'

Wordlessly, he took the brush and can from her hands. Set them firmly on the floor. 'You push a man too far…'

'Question is, how far?' He smelled of sweat and beer, his paint-smeared brow endearingly amusing. Keeping her eyes on his, she inched the fabric of his T-shirt upward, felt a spasm in unyielding muscle beneath her hand.

'…you're going to get burned,' he finished, though it was his voice that sounded singed. Like charred paper.

She watched his eyes turn a smoky blue, saw a single bead of sweat track down his forehead to disappear into his eyebrows. Was it her imagination or was he leaning closer?

One arm came up to rest beside her head, until all she could see was that incendiary blue gaze, all she could feel was his body heat grazing the front of her body.

'I love hot,' she said, and noticed her voice had dropped a notch. 'Chilli pepper. Saunas. Lying naked in front of an open fire till your—'

His mouth crashed down on hers. Fast, scorching. No

patience, no tenderness, just one touch and a fevered need
that flared to instant life between them.

Oh, yes. Her blood turned to syrup and her body sagged
against the wall. She'd known he'd taste like this. Potent,
powerful and hungry as he meshed those luscious lips with
hers, carnal pleasure that left her dizzy.

Deeper. She moaned into his mouth, willing more as his
lips pried hers apart and demanded entry. His tongue was
quick and clever, with dark desire and dangerous delights.
Desire for *her*.

The universe shifted, stars collided.

The woman inside her instinctively leaned closer, her
pelvis brushing against hard masculine arousal, her fingers
twisting in the soft folds of his T-shirt.

His hands slid down, over her waist, to cup her bottom
and pull her closer, then immediately rose again to fan out
over her ribcage, just below her breasts. Her mind emptied
of everything except Zak and how good he felt. How good
she felt. How good they felt together.

Then his fingers were clenching against her, his body
rigid with the strain, his breathing harsh as he lifted his
head. Shock darkened his eyes, furrowed his brow, as if he
couldn't quite comprehend what had happened.

Hell. Abruptly Zak stepped back, cursing the mind pictures Abby had painted that had pushed him to the edge.
Over the edge, he admitted, appalled.

'Why did you stop?'

Her breathless words had him cursing anew. 'One of us
had to,' he rasped.

'Why? You liked it. I liked it.'

He took in her glazed eyes, the lush temptation of her
mouth still damp from his, the rapid rise and fall of her
breasts. Oh, yeah, he liked. Too much. He wanted to do it

all over again, and more. To strip away those clothes and fill his hands with that soft female flesh. To lose himself inside that body and forget the pain of the past year.

But it wouldn't be fair. He would *not* use her to drown out the past or for his own lust. 'Believe me, we'd be wrong for each other.' He turned away and swiped up the brush she'd been using. 'I'll say it again: go to bed, Abby. I don't have time for distractions.'

All he could hear in the silence that followed was the sound of the sea matching his body's restless response. A tense silence. Enough time and silence to realise his words had offended, had hurt.

'You're right,' he heard her say at last. 'Workaholics aren't my type.'

Hurt or humiliation—perhaps both—trembled ever so slightly in her voice as she walked out, shutting the door behind her.

His fingers tightened on the brush, then he tossed it on the newspaper as he bent down to slam the lid on the paint tin. Dark emotion tortured him. If Diane had lived, if he knew the truth now about what had been going on behind his back—*or not*—maybe things could have been different between him and Abby.

Maybe.

He sat down on the trestle, resting his forearms on his knees, then remembered he'd not returned a message from Nick earlier in the evening. Probably to see if he'd lined up a date for the wedding yet. Zak could almost hear the conversation…

'Problem?' Nick would ask.

'Could be.'

'Does it have anything to do with a certain auburn-haired massage therapist who's great with kids and has you awake at night thinking crazy thoughts?'

Bingo.

'So again, what's the problem? Ask her. It's been over a year, Zak. An evening with an attractive woman…We know you and Di had a great marriage. She'd have wanted you to get out there again, be happy…'

Zak shuddered. Nick didn't know squat about Zak's marriage. No, he decided, as he dragged his soul-weary self off the trestle and headed for his room. He was going to the wedding alone.

The three hours' sleep Zak had managed hadn't improved his mood any. He pulled out the makings for breakfast. Abby's sense of fun had been… Okay, he admitted, it would have been fun…with a guy who appreciated it. Someone who could give as good as he got.

Once upon a time that man might have been him.

He slapped a pack of bacon on the bench. Yes, he was attracted to her spontaneity. Her open, caring nature.

The way she kissed.

A bolt of heat shot through his body. Oh, yeah, the sensation of her mouth against his—satin and sun. He cracked four eggs into a bowl. Scrambled, he decided, pulling out the whisk. Very scrambled. *Don't think.* Thoughts were dangerous. He might be tempted to be that fun guy again.

He glanced up at the ceiling. Hell, did he even remember how? One thing was damn certain: Abby didn't deserve his shabby dismissal.

He was sliding bacon onto the eggs when Abby appeared at the kitchen door in a fanciful lavender dress with sparkly bits on the bodice and hem and white knitted bolero. She looked fresh. Refreshed. How did she manage that on three hours' sleep?

'Good morning,' she said, as if they hadn't kissed each other senseless a few hours earlier.

'Good morning. You want breakfast?'

She nodded. 'Only if you have enough.'

'Coffee? Or would you prefer your witch's brew?'

'Coffee's fine.'

He caught two slices of toast as they popped up. 'Toast?'

'Please.'

The only sounds were the scratch of metal on toast as he buttered them and cut them into triangles. He flicked a switch and filled the silence with cheery breakfast radio, then carried the plates to the veranda.

Abby followed with the coffee. 'I've been thinking,' she said, sitting opposite him and pouring two mugs. She pushed his mug towards him and her gaze was bright and sure. 'And I've decided to focus on practicalities. Right now I need customers on my massage mat more than I need your problems with intimacy.'

His bite of toast lodged behind his Adam's apple. She always saw right through him, but this time she wasn't trying to fix it. He cleared his throat. 'About last night—'

'No.' She shook her head as she cut him off. 'We do not want to talk about last night. I'm going to the shop soon to finish setting up and I don't need the added stress.' Cool and firm and distant.

Understandably so. 'It's Sunday,' he said. She'd told him she was going to spend the day relaxing before opening her shop on Monday. 'And you're not dressed for work.'

She forked up some egg. 'You're a seven-day-a-week

guy, aren't you? And my choice of clothing's none of your concern.'

Her words were clipped, and deep in her soft grey eyes he saw an uncharacteristic melancholy that wrenched at his heart. This morning she wasn't the Abby he'd come to know, and he wanted the old Abby back. 'I'm going to the Numinbah Valley this morning,' he said. 'I'm doing a quote for Forrester Building Restorations. Come with me.'

The words were out before he could call them back. Someone on the radio was singing about being accidentally in love. He gulped down coffee. 'It's okay, you're busy—'

'How far is it?' She picked up a slice of crisp bacon in her fingers and nibbled.

'An easy drive, less than an hour. You'll still have time to do whatever you need this afternoon.'

'In that case, thank you, I'd like to come.'

'It's called "the green behind the gold",' Zak told Abby as they drove into the hinterland west of Surfers Paradise.

Abby could see why. They stopped near Tamborine Mountain's golf course to admire the view. Lush green slopes swept down to the clump of high rises in the distance and the misty Pacific Ocean beyond.

She kept her distance from Zak, kept their conversation light and *not* flirty. Whenever she raised a hand to touch his arm, whenever she was tempted to lean closer, she withdrew. His words came back at her. *We'd be wrong for each other*.

They stopped in a little town and while Zak met with the owner of a small café about some renovations Abby wandered the tourist shops—art galleries, crafts and antiques, souvenirs.

The gentle tinkle of wind chimes and the scent of

incense drew her to a New Age shop. From behind the counter, a woman in a sleeveless gown of crushed white velvet assessed Abby and, obviously recognising a kindred spirit, smiled and pointed to a sign in the window. Readings by Destiny. Sundays 10-4. 'Can I do a reading for you?'

'Oh…' She was so tempted. 'Not today. Thanks, Destiny, I'm waiting for someone.'

'Some crystals, then?' She drew Abby's attention to a multicoloured display.

'They're lovely. I'm afraid I can't afford them.' But she held up a pale amethyst on a silver chain. It didn't cost anything to look.

'Thought I'd find you here.'

Caught unawares by the familiar voice, Abby looked up to see Zak in the middle of the shop, framed by Native-American dream-catchers. She'd seen him less than half an hour ago; there was nothing different about him now. But, oh, her heart spun a giddy circle. Her fanciful Piscean nature spun impossible dreams.

She was falling in love with him.

Falling in love with a man who didn't want love.

'Your man.' She heard the smile in Destiny's voice but it seemed to be coming from a long way away.

'Ah…no,' Abby said, looking away, suddenly unable to hold his gaze. She would *not* let him see what Destiny already knew.

'It's not a question, it's an observation. She likes this amethyst.' Destiny handed Zak the chain. 'Not her birthstone, but it matches her dress.'

'It does,' Zak agreed.

'Try it on—see how it looks.'

'No.' Abby stepped back, unusually flustered. 'It was just a whim…'

But Zak was already stepping closer. Almost as close as last night. She could smell him. Familiar, enticing. Exciting. He was lifting her hair, sliding warm fingers around her neck to fasten the clasp.

So close that now she had nowhere else to look. But she refused to notice the way his eyes caught the light. Or the way that very clever mouth curved a little at the corners, not even when his dimples came out of hiding for a brief moment.

'Whimsical looks good on you.' The pads of his thumbs soothed the pulse in her neck that was fluttering like the wind chimes in the doorway. 'Whimsical *is* you. We'll take it,' he told Destiny without breaking eye contact. He pressed a thumb against Abby's lips when she would have refused and said, 'Let me, okay?'

'You sure I can't do a reading for you two?' Destiny said. 'I could do you together; two for the price of one.'

'No, thanks,' Zak answered for them both. 'Not today.' He straightened up, drew out his wallet. 'It's time for lunch.'

As if Abby felt like eating now. But she let him escort her to a little outdoor café while they listened to cicadas and soaked sunshine into their skin.

At least it gave her time to settle and decide that her epiphany wasn't going to change their relationship. The glass of wine helped, and the knowledge that tomorrow she'd be too busy to think about it.

'If you don't mind, I'll just finish up that quote…' He produced his laptop from his briefcase.

'I do mind, as a matter of fact.'

Her dress and the crystal glared back at her in his glasses but his lips curved. 'Two minutes. Your nose and shoulders are turning pink.' He leaned down, produced a bottle of sunscreen and set it on the table.

She lifted her brows in surprise as she looked at his sun-kissed neck. His bronzed skin was used to the climate. He'd packed it with her fair complexion in mind.

So let him mind a little more. She uncapped the bottle, rubbed some into her nose and cheeks. 'I can manage my nose. I can probably do my shoulders, too, but I'm going to interrupt you.' She held the bottle over his keyboard. 'You're too work-oriented.'

'A second business, house to renovate.' But he took the bottle from her hand and squeezed a dollop onto his fingertips. 'Turn around.'

She did as he asked, lifting her hair from her nape. And sucked in a breath at the first contact of cold lotion and warm fingers. Ignoring the fact that it was Zak's fingers, and that they were doing crazy things to her libido, she kept her attention on the conversation. 'Agreed, but I have an off switch. Are the rest of your family workaholics?'

'Dad was until he was forced to retire due to ill health. He built Forrester Building Restorations from scratch.'

'And you took over.'

'My brothers didn't want a bar of it—they moved to Sydney, which left me. I couldn't let Dad's life's work be all for nothing.'

'Family's important,' she agreed.

He recapped the bottle, slid it back in his bag, ditto his laptop. 'Was your foster-mother in business, too?'

'You may have heard of Aurora. She had an astrology column in the daily newspaper and regular segments on TV shows. But she guards her privacy. My foster-father had his own remedial-massage business.'

'The reason you got involved in massage therapy?'

'Yes. His dedication inspired me. I did courses, worked as his assistant. He died of a heart attack some years back.'

'I'm sorry,' he said. 'What about your sister? Don't you want to find her?'

'Of course, more than anything. But it takes money, and after all these years…' she shook her head as the age-old loss wrapped around her heart '…I don't think it's even possible.'

'Your foster-mother won't help?'

Abby stiffened at the unintentional slur. 'She would, without hesitation, but I wouldn't expect her to. So I've never told her about wanting to find my roots. I made a promise to myself never to ask for monetary assistance. I stand or fall on my own two feet. Always.'

'What's your sister's name?' His voice was low and tender and it made her ache.

'Hayley.' She shrugged. 'Who knows what name she goes by now? When Good Vibrations is making millions I'll find her.'

'Speaking of Good Vibes, do you have everything you need for the big opening tomorrow?'

Abby nodded. 'Tina's in for a session tomorrow morning. And I have a couple of bookings for the afternoon. Tina says she needs some relaxation therapy before the wedding preparations start.'

He seemed surprised she knew and hesitated before saying, 'Yes, it's getting hectic. The wedding's weekend after next.'

'She tells me it's on a private island north of here.'

'That's right.'

'You're going, of course.'

'Yes.' He reached for his beer, avoiding eye contact.

'Good. That's good,' she said, when what she really wanted to know was if he was taking a Friend. She concentrated on keeping her expression casual and not thinking about Zak with a woman. 'You need a break.' Her voice sounded a bit high, a bit brittle.

His eyes followed a young couple enjoying one of Tamborine Mountain's carriage joy rides. 'Unfortunate timing with the centre just getting started, but it's only overnight.'

'Yes. Overnight.' She decided now was as good a time as any to say, 'I hope you won't mind, but Tina's invited me to the wedding, too.'

CHAPTER EIGHT

IN the run up to the wedding Zak was busy with renovations. He finished the second bathroom for Abby's use, and the living room looked comfortable with the new furniture and wide-screen TV. One day he might even have time to turn it on.

At Tina's invitation, Abby was going to the wedding. Abby's explanation was that there'd been a last-minute cancellation—but Abby didn't know it was his decision not to bring a partner that had resulted in the vacancy.

One of life's little ironies.

Even though he hadn't seen as much of Abby since that night in the living room when he'd all but lost control, reminders were never far away. If she wasn't steaming up his bathroom with enticing feminine scents or concocting delicious-smelling dishes in his kitchen, it was her multi-hued and very brief undergarments drying on the line.

She'd packed a picnic tea complete with candles one evening and they'd eaten it on the beach. He simply hadn't had the heart to say no. On another occasion she'd somehow secured his help applying *rainbow icing*, for heaven's sake, to a batch of chocolate-chip cookies for the office staff.

Since the painting incident, she hadn't pushed him towards anything intimate, but nonetheless something bordering on intimacy came out of their short times together. He felt…connected, in a way he'd never experienced before.

Abby was so different from any other woman he knew. And she seemed to know him, often better than he knew himself. Sometimes when she looked at him with those silver eyes he wanted to lash out at what had gone so horribly wrong with his marriage. He wanted to bury past hurts and mistakes and start over. With Abby.

But that was impossible.

He owed Diane. Some kind of self-sacrifice was her due, and his punishment.

Abby had made the journey to the island with the other guests, first by bus, then on the luxury yacht Nick and Tina had chartered with a scrumptious luncheon while on board. But Zak wasn't amongst them—he'd hired a helicopter to save time and was unloading his bag as they arrived.

Abby broke from the guests to meet him as he stepped from the floating helipad, the down-draught plucking at his hair as the helicopter rose, its blades chopping noisily through the air. His face was set in stern lines, his eyes hidden behind dark glasses. But she knew when he caught sight of her by the way the hairs on her arms lifted and her heart beat that little bit faster. She was practically out of breath when they met up.

The harsh expression softened. 'Good trip?' he asked.

'Wonderful. You?'

'Not bad.'

'Apparently we're going to be neighbours.' She waved to a clump of dwellings surrounded by palms near the water's edge that the wedding planner had indicated. 'We've got the villas closest to the beach, numbers eight and nine.' *Couldn't get much closer without sharing the same oxygen.*

And that thought must have registered in Zak's mind, too, because his smile dimmed a little. 'Better check it out, then.'

Since that kiss in the living room, she'd allowed Zak space while drawing him into simple activities and concentrating on Good Vibrations, which was starting to attract plenty of customers. He'd seemed happier, more at ease in their shared space, but tonight… She shook the thought away. They were here for a wedding, it wasn't a date.

The doors were unlocked and Abby took the first one. *Villa* was a relative term, she discovered. The little huts were constructed with wood and native palm. A panel opened to provide a window and let in air.

She swung her bag onto a simple bed. Mosquito netting suspended from the ceiling was draped to one side.

'If you need anything…' He nodded to a rattan-type door.

'Ah…the bathroom?'

'Afraid not. It's my room.' And he didn't look thrilled about it.

'You've been here before, then?'

He nodded once. 'The ablutions blocks are alongside the house. The island's not a regular tourist resort, and it only caters to twenty people, tops. The rest of the guests are sleeping on the launch tonight.'

'Okay.' Barely a screen separating them. And so small, so close, Abby had no doubt she'd hear him breathing, hear his body sliding over the sheets. If they had come as a couple…

But she told herself again, she was not Zak's wedding date. She was only here at Tina's invitation. She unzipped her bag. Its sharp rasping sound split the silence.

'I hope you'll have a good time while we're here,' Zak said. As stiff and formal as the suit he was about to put on.

'What about you? Are you going to let yourself enjoy a well-deserved break?' Frustrated at his non-reply, she turned away, pulled her slinky green dress out of her bag.

The one with the go-as-low-as-you-dare bodice.

'You're wearing that,' he said slowly into a sudden thick silence. She replayed Zak's reaction to seeing her in her emerald dress at the photo shoot. He'd looked as out of breath as she'd felt when she'd locked eyes with him across the room.

He looked that way again now. Only sterner.

'I am. Loosen up, Zak. It's only a dress.' *A dress designed to be taken off. Slowly. An inch at a time.* She slipped off her sandals, reached for the sparkly stilettos. Her anklet jangled as she stepped into them. 'Should I wear these, do you think? Are we going to be standing in sand?'

He looked down at her feet, his eyes flared a fraction as his gaze lingered on her ankles. 'I think there's a paved area…'

'If I fall, you'll catch me, right?' Her body heated at the memory of the last time she'd overturned an ankle—his hands on her as he'd lifted her to the trestle, the feel of his hard body against her breasts.

'I doubt it will come to that.' Clenching his bag, he crossed the room, wrenched the flimsy door open. 'Let me know when you're ready.'

Zak in a suit. Abby bit back the sigh when she opened her door later and saw him adjusting the cuffs while he waited on the path for her. Its dark fabric with accompanying white shirt accentuated his tanned skin as he watched the wedding party assemble.

'I'm ready.'

He turned at the sound of her voice. The setting sun behind him obscured his features and made him look like some sort of divine haloed being.

'That dress… The colour suits you.' His face might be in shadow, but she could feel the hot caress of those eyes over the fabric. Feminine satisfaction slid through her; she knew she'd wowed him. She was tempted to touch the zip between her breasts to check it wasn't too revealing, but decided it might draw his attention there and now wasn't the time. Instead she fluffed her hair. She'd left it down since Zak liked it that way.

He stepped towards her. 'Shall we join the others?'

When he offered his arm the gesture warmed Abby from the inside out. Even though said arm was as tense as twined wire across a suspension bridge. 'You mean, like we're partners?'

He hesitated. 'If that's what you'd like.'

She smiled, encouraged, sure the blush of surprise and happiness showed in her cheeks. Maybe, just maybe, her attempts to draw Zak out of himself were starting to pay off. 'I would.'

He nodded. 'Let's go, then.'

They might have been any two people out for a romantic sunset stroll. She hugged his arm, her hand brushing against the fabric of his suit as she inhaled his refreshed cologne.

The last rays of the sun seemed to surround the bride and groom and their loved ones. Crimson and orange painted the clear sky and reflected on the water. Tina looked radiant in an off-the-shoulder apricot organza gown shimmering in the gentle breeze, her skin bronzed by the sunset.

After the simple ceremony, a buffet dinner was served

on the veranda of the main house. The band played as Nick and Tina performed their own interpretation of the bridal waltz over the temporary dance floor. Soon other couples were joining in.

'You want to give it a try?' Abby asked as Zak watched the dancers with a beer bottle in his hand.

'Maybe later.'

Yeah. By the remote look in his eyes he meant much later. When the band packed up, more like. What had happened to the Zak who'd greeted her at the villa not more than two hours ago? 'Let me know if you change your mind.' Determined not to show her disappointment, she walked away to mingle with the other guests and perhaps drum up some business in the process.

Whenever Abby turned she found herself glancing at a familiar pair of blue eyes. More often than not they flicked away, but occasionally they lingered for heart-pounding seconds at a time, as if daring her. Or daring himself. It was like a game in itself.

This time, however, she could see him across the dance floor, grinning at something someone said, but his grin vanished as their gazes met and held, and something powerful seemed to open up between them. The rest of the guests seemed to melt away, leaving only the two of them and a shimmering pool of promise—

'Remember me?' interrupted a smooth, masculine, alcohol-imbued voice beside her.

Reluctantly, she dragged her attention away. 'You're Nick's cousin.' She forced a smile at the guy with poster-boy good looks, trying not to be annoyed at the interruption, trying to remember his name and trying to pinpoint exactly what it was she found disturbing about him.

'Vince.'

'Ah, yes.' She took a sip of her drink, cast a quick glance about, but Zak seemed to have disappeared. 'How's it going, Vince?'

'Couldn't be better.' His perfect smile gleamed as his somewhat glazed eyes travelled over her body. She could almost hear his brain cells figuring how long it would take to get the zip down and the garment off.

He tipped his beer bottle to his lips, took a long draught. 'How about a twirl on the dance floor?'

Abby was tempted, just for a minute, to see if it would coax Zak into some sort of action and enjoying himself a little, but the thought of letting Poster Boy get his hands on her changed her mind. 'What about your partner for the evening?'

For a beat out of time something dark lurked in the depths of his eyes, sending a shiver down Abby's spine, then it was gone and his mouth tilted in a lazy grin. 'I came alone. No attachments.' His bottle glinted in the lights as he raised it above his head. 'Live for the moment, I say.' He downed the remainder of his beer. 'So…what say we seize that moment?'

Without realising it, she'd stepped back. 'Thanks, but I promised Zak the first dance.'

'Zak?' He shook his head. 'Trouble with Forrester is he doesn't know how to have a good time.' He reached for Abby but she slipped away, her fingers clenched around the stem of her wineglass.

'Abby, ready for that dance?' Zak materialised beside her, and before she could react he pried the glass from her fingers, set it on a nearby table, then nodded to Poster Boy. 'Vince.'

With the lightest touch, he set a hand at the small of her back and steered her away from Vince towards the dance floor. Even though his fingertips were only a whisper against her silk dress, her heart danced to its own little steps. Those fingers might be barely touching but the *way* they touched... Protective, possessive. As if he were *jealous*?

Someone was lighting kerosene torches amongst the tables and the band switched to dreamy island music. The men had long since dispensed with jackets and ties and rolled up their sleeves.

Abby looked up and saw the flush rising up Zak's neck and slid a hand over one of his. 'Prove him wrong, Zak. Start enjoying yourself.'

Zak uncurled the hand enclosed in Abby's and rotated it so that their palms met and linked his fingers through hers. *Damn Vince.* No way was he letting him get his hands on Abby. Even if she wasn't Zak's partner. Even if he'd had no intention of dancing.

Abby leaned closer, so that her face was all he could see, so that he could smell the sweet pineapple meringue she'd been eating, and said, 'We can go for a walk along the beach instead if you'd rather.'

Oh, yeah, the possibilities *that* suggestion conjured... But, for now, he set his free hands on the satin-smooth curve of her waist. 'Who says we can't do both?'

He slid his hand behind her, working his way up her spine and under the silky tumble of fragrant hair. Wrong move. With a lurching sense of dread, he knew he'd been deceiving himself. It wasn't just the dance or the fact that he wanted to stake his claim for Vince's—or anyone else's—eyes. It was pure possessiveness.

He had no right to feel its burn, so he had no right to hold her close enough that their legs entwined and her breasts slid against his shirt. Close enough to see the steady pulse above the tempting line of her collarbone.

'It's working.' She nodded to where Vince was watching them with an arm slung round a brunette's shoulders, then turned her gaze to Zak.

And everything in his mind vanished. Falling into her silver eyes hadn't been his intention. The torchlight glowed on her skin, glistened on the tiny beads of perspiration dotting her brow. He'd been right: in her high heels she lined up against him perfectly.

Now the patter of island drums in the background echoed to the beat in his ears, the throb in his groin. Stepping back from the too-close contact, he wished there were a jukebox handy or an upbeat rock band so they could move together without the necessity of touching.

And Vince was still watching.

'Stay clear of Nick's cousin,' he advised. 'He's a serial womaniser.'

Abby's smile dimmed a little. 'It's a smokescreen.'

He choked back a short four-letter word. 'You don't know him.'

'I know him better than you think.' She shook her head, setting her long silver and emerald crystal earrings jangling, and the smile returned. 'And I can take care of myself.'

He reckoned she could, and immediately regretted spilling his thoughts and hoped he didn't sound like a jealous lover. He replaced his hands on Abby's waist, but resisted the instinctive urge to let them roam again.

'Mmm, that's nice.' She slid her arms up his chest and, closing the gap he'd created between them, hooked her arms around his neck and massaged little circles at the base of his skull with her fingers. As if she belonged there.

She was looking at him with such hope, her eyes seemed to say, *You're changing, and I like what I see.* He liked the changes, too. He liked the way she made him feel. Too much.

'I think Tina approves,' she whispered against his cheek.

He glanced about them. She was right, he noted with a scowl of annoyance at the subtle glances being cast their way. Worse, the increasingly obvious desire throbbing low in his body was threatening to become the next topic of conversation.

'So…' Smiling, she lifted a shoulder and shifted, so close all he could see was the glint of mischief in her eyes. 'Shall we give all the women something to really knock their stilettos off?'

He smiled back. Why, he had no idea; shock perhaps— because it wasn't remotely amusing, but damned if his body wasn't tensing up in anticipation.

'Relax…' Her hands slid to cup his jaw, smoothing a thumb over his dimple as her lips curved. Then she surprised the hell out of him by planting her mouth, not on his as he expected, but there, in the hollow on his left cheek. He felt its petal softness, the dab of moisture, the lingering pressure before she pulled back.

And all he could think was how her mouth would feel, how it would taste against his.

An extroverted voice cut across the music and out of the corner of his eye he caught sight of Vince as he twirled his partner, this time a long-legged blonde, onto the dance floor.

Zak didn't spare them a glance. His lips itched with wanting, Abby's scent seeped into every pore of his suddenly very hot, very hard body.

He leaned towards her and her lips met his halfway. Not the same tentative mouth that had grazed his cheek, but hotter, firmer, richer. And that same vibrant energy that always accompanied everything she did flowed from her kiss and into him.

A murmured groan rumbled from deep in his solar

plexus and rose up his throat. He didn't want to feel the heat, the tension, this excruciating awareness that twined like silken ropes around him, binding and confining... He reared back and found himself pinned by her gaze.

Then her lips were on his again and his mind shut down. He couldn't think of anything at all. All he was capable of was feeling. And it felt damned good.

Nothing had felt this good in a very long time.

He absorbed the sensations of warmth, understanding and intimacy, reawakening every dormant desire he'd ever had. Every fantasy he'd imagined about Abby since she'd stormed into his life.

She touched him with the assurance of a long-term lover, letting her hands roam over his face and shoulders, and he yielded to her gentle insistence and the soothing murmur in her throat, opening up and letting go.

Somewhere in the back of his mind his conscience hammered at him, reminding him that he was indulging in the moist warmth of her kiss, the satin smoothness of her skin, and warning him that this pleasure could only be temporary.

Temporary insanity, perhaps, because nothing should feel this right.

When he felt her pulling back he wanted to howl at the star-studded sky, *Not yet!* Tangling his hands in the fruit-fragrant tresses of her hair, he held her head still and deepened the kiss. She tasted sweet yet tart, like ripening apples, a temptation no man could resist.

He couldn't remember why he should. His hands moved to her ears to feel the cool silver jewellery against the warmth of her skin. To her jaw, the pulse in her neck beating beneath his fingertips. To cover her hands, which were moving and flexing against his chest.

His ears registered the change in tempo as the band

switched to some sort of fast salsa. Hot, like the woman pressed against him. Like the lava bubbles crackling through his veins.

Finally, as breathless as if he'd danced the salsa himself, he raised his head, shook it to check if the world had tilted or if it was just him. A giddy carousel of colour and movement gyrated about them, but all he saw was Abby. Her hair tangled around her face like errant flames—his handiwork—and her eyes blazed with the same wildfire.

She let out a deep unsteady breath. 'I think we've made our point. Hardly a stiletto in sight.' She laughed, sounding as out of breath as he.

True, he noted, most women had tossed away their shoes to dance barefoot. Abby's eyes, luminous in the orange glow, melted into his. 'So…what do you suggest now?'

Was it a trick of the flickering torchlight or the buzzing in his ears or was Abby imagining what he was imagining? Two naked and writhing bodies burning up the sheets on a single bed a scant fifty metres away.

'That walk you mentioned earlier.' Taking her hand, he headed away from the party and noise and heat, towards the cooler palm-shadowed path.

But despite his inner plea for the sake of self-preservation, the carnal, earthy image of the two of them continued to smoulder behind his eyes and smoke in his blood. The million-dollar question now was how was he going to keep his lips—and his hands—to himself for the rest of the evening?

Darkness hid a multitude of sins. He was grateful for it as he towed Abby along the path where the edge of the sand was dappled with starlight beneath leafy palms. The front of his trousers felt two sizes too tight; he needed the salty air near the ocean to cool off.

'Wait up,' a breathless voice gasped as they neared the villas.

He felt the tug on his hand. Only then did he realise he'd been so focused on his own predicament and how close he was to the edge of control that he hadn't spared Abby a glance. He came to an immediate halt. 'Sorry.'

'Shoes are rubbing,' she apologised, wrapping her hand around his forearm for balance while she rubbed her toes through the straps.

'Why didn't you take them off?'

'Pure vanity. I've never had such gorgeous sexy shoes and I wanted—'

'Well, take them off now. No one's here to see.'

Her eyes flicked to his. 'You are.' The velvet caress of her voice slid through him, but she leaned down and un-strapped them, slid them off. 'Trouble is I have very sensi-tive feet. Ticklish as hell and when someone touches my—'

'You're bleeding,' he said, cutting off any images in-volving her feet and touching before they could take shape in his mind while he frowned at the twin blood-stained blisters on her smallest toes.

'I'm fine.' She picked up her shoes, her voice turning to velvet again as she said, 'What I want to know is where to from here?'

'One thing's for sure, it's not walking on the sand—not with the state of those blisters.'

'No, it's not.'

And his body swelled and hardened with the knowl-edge.

She stepped in front of him, so close that he could feel her breath on his face. The air between them grew tense and heavy, throbbing in time with the distant band and his thickening pulse.

Her eyes were dark in the leafy dimness but wide and aware as they stroked down his body, over every hard and aching inch, and back to his. Eyes that saw too much, knew too much.

The shoes slipped from her fingers and landed with a thud, like the sound of a door closing. Or another opening… She set her palms against his chest, their heat searing him through the soft weave of his shirt as they travelled up to his shoulders. Then hotter, closer as they dipped beneath his open collar to gently knead and squeeze taut muscles.

'You're as hard as iron,' she murmured.

And he could tell by the awareness that burned in her eyes that she knew exactly how hard he was, and where.

'Let me help you, Zak.'

He inhaled sharply, only to drag in a lungful of her perfume.

Let her help?

Let her put those hands on his neck? His back? Or did she mean on other, more needy places? Was it only hands she meant? As the questions spun through his mind he struggled to contain the renewed tide of something akin to fear surging through him. He'd always prided himself on his control.

Dragging his gaze from her solemn eyes and the tempting sight of those full lips only a sigh away from his, he searched the horizon where a few sparse mainland lights glimmered like tiny jewels. And it occurred to him: over the water was his reality, but here…this island was a time-out. An oasis in the desert that was his emotional life right now. *Just for tonight…*

'Okay, forget I spoke.' Her hands slid away and he heard her resignation as she bent to retrieve her shoes.

Instantly the skin she'd touched turned cold and he wished he could call back the moment, recapture a fleeting fragment of that connection. A connection he knew they'd both felt, and acknowledged.

'Let's go back to the party, then,' he heard her say.

He waited until she straightened, then looked into her eyes and made his decision: *one night*. 'No.'

CHAPTER NINE

BLINKING, Abby did a double-take as she looked up into Zak's eyes. And one swift hard spike of adrenaline spurted along her veins. This was The Look. The look that said he was finally going to act on what had been building between them over the past weeks.

The bunching of muscles along his jaw, the almost imperceptible way his lips softened and parted as he drew in an unsteady breath. And, most telling of all, the hot, hot spark that glittered behind those heavy-lidded eyes.

One spark to turn her into a smouldering mass of need. It had been a long time since she'd experienced anything remotely intimate. Just standing within Zak's sphere of potent masculine energy, breathing in his musky, turned-on scent and sharing this amazing eye contact was more intimate than anything she'd shared with another man.

She'd caught glimmers of that look in his eyes before, but this time he didn't turn away. Her heart pounded in her ears, her whole body turned lethargic and fluid, and she wanted to lean against his body and melt into his skin.

He didn't give her time—ironic since he'd spent the past couple of weeks in slow motion—and, grabbing her hand, he strode along the path to their villas, her sore feet obviously forgotten. Seemed once he'd made up his mind there was no stopping him.

They reached her door first. It was unlocked and he pushed it open. The scents of hibiscus and rattan matting wafted out on the evening air. They stepped inside. The glow from the torches outside painted a gold patina over his skin, deepening the grooves in his face.

His breathing was laboured, his gaze harsh and unforgiving as he turned to look at her.

'Perhaps we need to…' She trailed off as his eyes opened and bored into hers, hot with conflicting emotions that, even with the people skills she prided herself on, she couldn't read. 'You have problems with intimacy. Whoever she was, she really laid one on you, didn't she?'

He flinched but didn't reply.

Her voice softened as she said, 'You don't have to do anything you don't feel ready for.'

His lips twisted in a flash of wry amusement at odds with the tortured eyes. 'Isn't that the guy's line?'

A laugh bubbled up. 'Anyone'd think you're a virgin.' She stared back at those eyes and the laughter died. 'You're not, are you?'

His smile eased the tension a fraction. 'No.'

She let out a quietly relieved breath and lit the lavender-scented candle she'd set by her bed to soothe her to sleep later. 'If you just want to talk about…whatever…we can do that.'

'Talk?' The rough sound that erupted from his throat had her turning. 'No, Abby, I don't want to talk.' He pushed the light-framed rattan door closed, leaned his head against it. His eyes flicked shut then opened almost immediately, his fingers fisting at his sides. 'Damn it.'

She saw the way his shoulders hunched, watched the

rise and fall of his chest as he took a deep breath. 'I'm sorry if I make you uncomfortable.'

'Too flaming right you make me uncomfortable.' He shot a disparaging glance downward then his eyes rocked back to hers. 'In too many ways to count. And here's the thing. All I can see when I shut my eyes is *you*.'

Abby caught the bouquet he'd tossed her, thorns and all. What she saw was a man in emotional turmoil.

'That's a backhanded compliment if ever I heard one. I'll try not to be offended.' She moved to the foot of the bed and unzipped her overnighter. 'Sit on the edge of the bed.'

She unearthed her bottle of body lotion from her toiletry bag. 'Oils are better, but this'll do for now.' When she turned, he hadn't moved from his spot by the door. She tilted the bottle towards him. 'A little relaxation therapy. Free of charge.' She felt her half-smile drop away and her own body tensed as she took in the state of his arousal, the way his eyes darkened to almost cobalt in the candlelight as she lifted her gaze to his. 'You'll sleep better.'

He made a guttural sound in his throat. 'Sleep?'

'Later,' she promised. *Much later.* She crossed the room to close the window's rattan panel and shut the rest of the world out.

By the time she'd double-checked the door, poured a glass of water from her bottle on the bedside table, he'd complied with her request and was sitting on the bed, knuckles white on either side of his tense thighs.

'Have a drink first.' She offered him the water.

'Thanks.'

Her gaze was drawn to the way his mouth touched the glass, the long tendons in his neck as he swallowed, the moisture on his upper lip when he lowered the glass. Her own mouth ached to kiss that moisture away, to elicit a smile at the very least. But Zak wasn't big on smiling right now.

When he'd had enough she took the glass from his hands, and, without breaking eye contact, turned it so that her lips touched the rim where his mouth had been. His eyes dropped to her mouth and he swallowed audibly. In the warm flickering light the atmosphere turned sultry, beating with the desire that pulsed through her body.

She set the glass down, resisted the urge to lick her lips. 'Okay,' she said, striving for a light tone in the heavy silence. 'Work with me here. And don't look so serious; this is supposed to be a pleasant experience.'

She knelt in front of him, began untying his laces. 'I'm just going to remove your shoes…' Her pulse tripped as she slipped off his shoes, then his socks and, oh, his feet— long, long toes that flexed and arched beneath her touch. Like feet in the throes of passion…

She squirted a dollop of lotion onto her palms, rubbed them together. Using the flats of her hands, she worked slowly from his ankles and down the front of his feet. Focusing her gaze on the task rather than the smoky depths of his eyes on hers or the fact that the musky curve of his neck was a tempting nuzzle away…

'Close your eyes and think about the stress flowing out through your feet.'

Relax? Let the stress flow out? Under other circumstances, Zak might have laughed at the sheer impossibility. But he was in no mood for laughter. Or talk, for that matter. How the hell did one relax with one's body tight and hot and so pumped he was all but vaulting out of his skin?

Think? He couldn't think about anything but the silky moist touch of her hands, or the fact that he knew she wasn't wearing a bra beneath that dress. That one tug on her zipper and he could bury his face in that sweet shadowed valley between her breasts.

His body tightened painfully. He closed his eyes as instructed only to have them flash open again when he felt her shift as her hands moved to the front of his shirt and began undoing buttons.

Knuckles grazing his chest as she worked her way lower, spreading the sides of his shirt wide. Warm fingers catching in chest hair, and—he sucked in a taut breath—fingernails wreaking havoc as they scored over his nipples. *Intentionally?* 'What are you doing?'

Her eyes met his, honestly and openly, and he could see she was no longer Abby the professional therapist, but Abby, the woman, and that she was as pumped as he.

'I'm removing your shirt,' she said. The silk-over-sand voice—meant to soothe? Or to seduce. Tugging the shirt free of his trousers, she slid her moisture-slick palms over his shoulders and down his arms, taking the fabric with them. Until he was naked from the waist up.

His exposed skin prickled with heat as her breath fanned his cheek, his neck, his upper chest, her unique fragrance and the underlying almost-forgotten scent of woman whirled through his head till he was dizzy.

'This isn't working,' he said, reeling at the thick, turned-on sound of his own voice.

'You're right.' She rocked back on her heels. 'Maybe some other time.'

'No.' A storm of emotions whipped through him. 'Tonight's all there is.' All he'd let it be.

Her solemn eyes locked with his, shimmering in the candlelight. 'If that's your choice.'

No, a voice inside him yelled. 'It is.'

She nodded, then capped her bottle and rose, turning away to place it on the night-stand.

No! Hell. She didn't understand, this evening, the single solitary one he'd allowed himself—them—wasn't over, it was just beginning. Panic swamped him; the restless, insistent need to finish what they'd started pounded through his blood. He jerked up off the bed. 'Abby…'

He heard her breath catch as he moved behind her. At the touch of his fingers on her nape, over her neck, her throat. Her skin was as smooth as polished stone yet soft, warm.

'I'm too strung out for a massage,' he said, against her ear. He continued to play his fingers over her shoulders and down her arms, imagining them playing in other, more intimate places. Her hair tickled his nose: an orchard in spring with a blend of blossom and fruit.

He wanted to taste her skin, right there on her neck just below her ear. And he didn't want to stop there. He ached to taste all her hidden secrets, to lose himself inside her and just for one night to forget the world outside the two of them existed.

In a way it was a relief she couldn't see him because he had a hunch this hunger for her was inscribed in neon over his face, and that was a vulnerability he could do without. She must never see how deeply she got to him.

'I think you misunderstood.' To demonstrate, he set his open mouth on her shoulder and tilted his pelvis against her spine. And, ah, she tasted as he knew she'd taste: a blend of sweet and tart, the way her lips had when he'd kissed her. A shudder ran through him, or her, he wasn't sure who.

'On the contrary,' he heard her say through the drumming in his ears, 'I understand you very well.' If she hadn't turned in his arms he would have missed seeing the hot flare of molten silver in her eyes because her voice was carefully neutral when she said, 'You need a woman.'

No. He didn't. He'd been doing fine up till a couple of weeks ago. He needed… '*You*, Abby.'

That admission, that open acknowledgement, spun through the air, a mutual aphrodisiac, a mutual acceptance.

Their eyes locked, he sucked in a breath as her fingers busied themselves with his belt buckle. Held that breath as she deftly lowered the zipper in his trousers. Nearly exploded as her knuckles deliberately caressed his erection, and again when she slid her hands down his hips and over his thighs, until his trousers hit the floor.

Her eyes flicked down to the tent in his boxers, then back to his. 'You want me to do the honours?'

Yes— No! If she removed them the way she'd removed his trousers, the main event would be over before he'd got started.

And, 'Hardly equable—I'll be the only one naked.'

Her lips pouted, a sensual pucker as she said, 'That's not a turn-on for you?'

He looked down at himself, back to her. 'It's fair to say I don't need turning on.'

Her gaze slid over his erection. 'You're right.' Her voice lowered. 'What now?'

What now? Keep it slow. You're only going to get one chance at this. 'We'll try it my way.'

Without waiting for a response, he pirouetted her, stepping back until the backs of his thighs hit the bed. And not a moment too soon. He sank down gratefully. His legs felt as if they'd run a marathon.

With hands almost as unsteady he drew her between his legs so that her body was flush against him, her pelvic bones rubbing where he burned for her the most. Her dress a silky whisper against his inner thighs, her heat seeping into his body until he reached flashpoint.

He reached out. A rustle as he untied the bow, another as he tugged the zipper, just a tantalising inch, revealing creamy flesh, lightly freckled, like her face. Natural beauty. She didn't cover it up under a truckload of make-up like other women he knew. What you saw was what you got.

Just Abby. He eased the zip down further—*slowly*—refusing to give in to the urgency pounding through his bloodstream.

Slid his palms between silk and skin. Gliding his hands under the swell of her breasts. Around. And, ah…over the hard little peaks that rose like buds in the sunshine against his palms. Her breath hitched. Scarcely able to breathe himself, he parted the fabric, wanting to see what his hands were touching.

His mouth turned dry, his blood sizzled. More smooth pale skin, large rosy nipples that begged for his attention. 'That dress doesn't do you justice.' He lowered the zip all the way, revealing a compact navel, the dips and valleys of her woman's body, gold and violet in the candlelight.

He couldn't wait. He had to lay his lips against her and taste. Had to slide his tongue over the perfect mounds, to take one of those peaks into his mouth, tug on it with his teeth until she moaned. Until it wasn't enough. He let his teeth scrape over her one more time, then pulled away. 'You're beautiful.'

Shrugging the fabric off her shoulders, she slithered out of the dress and stood before him wearing nothing but a teasing minuscule scrap of green lace and ribbon. Her eyes were watching his when he finally raised them. 'So are you,' she said, and leaned down, cupped his jaw in her hand. Then her lips were on his, cool and firm, soothing their heat, stoking the fire lower down.

Ah, when was the last time he'd felt this primed, this hot, this ready?

'Stand up, Abby.'

She leaned back, her eyes on his, then uncoiled herself in a slow sinuous motion that had his tongue all but hanging out.

'I want to look at you.' He slid his fingers beneath the straps on her hips, then watched the thong slither down the long, long length of her thighs, her calves, over her anklet to the floor.

She was perfect. And he wanted to explore all that perfection, starting at her toes and working his way up. But her feet were too far away. His hand slid between her thighs—much closer—to her warm waiting heat. A slow glide and his thumb found the throbbing nub of her pleasure.

'Zak…' She sighed and arched closer.

When her knees buckled, he dragged her closer with a murmured, 'Come here,' and settled her on his thighs, legs parted, exposing her to his gaze.

Lust hummed like bees as his fingers slid over and over against her wetness. His eyes flicked to hers. Glazed, and passion-bright, they melted into his as she clutched at his shoulders, her inner muscles clenched tight around his fingers, drawing him deep, her rippling climax turning his lust to desperation. 'Abby.'

Shucking his underwear, he pulled her up, and backwards onto the bed, dragging her body over every aching inch of his until she sprawled, gasping, on top of him. Her hair brushed his shoulders, her lips and sighs caressed his face, his eyes, an ear. And the friction of her skin against his was like nothing he'd ever felt before. The tip of his erection rubbed like oiled silk against her still quivering heat—

'Zak…' A hand slid between them in the same instant that he remembered. 'Wait…'

Protection.

His runaway hormones screeched to a halt. Everything inside him howled, *Ignore it*, the driving urge to completion pounded in his groin, thundered through his veins. *'Hell.'* Hell, hell, hell.

Abby's wide-eyed gaze locked with his. 'Oh.'

They stared at each other, heavy breath mingling, sweat-sheened bodies pounding in unison. 'Sex was the last thing on my mind when we left Surfers.' A downright lie. He just hadn't intended acting on it.

A wordless message, an erotic heat, shimmered in her eyes. Then she pushed up, knelt beside him on the narrow bed.

And her gaze drifted down.

The air constricted in his lungs, his throat closed over and anticipation surged through him. He ground his teeth till they ached. Not that. Too personal, too intimate. 'No,' he muttered, clutching the sheet either side of him, but his body had other ideas.

'Let me.' She splayed a hand on his chest.

Everything else faded to black.

All he saw was Abby. All he knew was Abby. The scent of her arousal mingling with the fragrance of her skin, her taste on his lips. Her feminine appreciation shivering through him in hot and cold bursts as she caressed his body with eyes and hands and murmurs. Soft and sweet, slow and seductive.

Then she took him into the wet heat of her mouth and his mind and the world as he knew it spun out of control.

On a groan, his eyes rolled back, his lids fell closed. Yes! The feel of her tongue as it skimmed and swirled— 'No!'

he rasped, reaching down between his thighs, catching her face with trembling hands.

She lingered a moment, her eyes on his, then let him go, replaced her mouth with her hands and soothed, 'Okay.'

His head flopped back onto the pillow as she slithered upward. The world would never be the same again. He and Abby could never be the same again. The woman who was pumping him, holding him as he came, as he spilled into her palms. He gripped her shoulders as the force of his climax shuddered through him.

A husky voice breathed his name near his ear a moment later. He couldn't help it—his hand trailed across the smoothness of her shoulder, a breast, her belly as he slid it down towards hers, but she batted it away.

'I'll take care of it,' she murmured.

He closed his eyes.

'You okay?' she whispered.

'Yeah. Great.' Just great. He forestalled any further communication by angling away from her. Guilt wound through the remnants of his pleasure.

'Good.' She patted his arm.

A few moments later, he felt her slide down beside him again. He kept his eyes closed. Gradually the sensual fog cleared, his senses calmed enough to pick up on his cramped surroundings.

Abby's head nestled in his armpit, her breath streaming over his chest as she settled towards sleep. One of his legs dangled over the edge of the bed. He could smell the lavender candle, hear the languorous lap of the sea outside, the faraway sound of party-goers, the annoying buzz of a mosquito near his head.

What they'd done played once more through his head. Even if they hadn't completed the sexual act, somehow what they'd done seemed more intimate. He didn't know why, couldn't explain it. Nor did he want to explain it. Perhaps it was the fact that she'd obviously enjoyed it as much as he.

He'd have to move in a moment. Couldn't leave a candle burning, and he should drape the mosquito netting around them.

His eyes blinked open. *Them?* Every muscle froze in denial. No! No way was he sleeping in Abby's bed with the physical reminder of what they'd shared. The more emotional—and timely—reminder that this was a one-off.

Then he realised the candle was already extinguished. So he lay still, waiting for the slow deep breathing that would tell him Abby had fallen asleep and he could get up and go to his own room without the necessity of speaking further. Telling her it was the closest he'd felt to another human being in a long time. Years, in fact. Crazy.

Diane was the woman he loved. *Had* loved. Abby wasn't his kind of woman. And the laughter he heard wasn't the demon on his shoulder telling him he was a fool and why couldn't he just admit the fact that Abby not only turned him on, she turned him inside out? With need, desire and a whole lot of other emotions he refused to analyse.

He gritted his teeth and stared at the ceiling in the dimness. No, the noise was some drunken party guest enjoying a walk along the shoreline.

But he could talk to Abby in a way he'd never been able to with his wife. Unlike Diane, Abby's moods didn't swing with the wind and she meant what she said and said what she meant. She understood and cared about other people, even had a charitable word to say for Vince—what was it she sensed about a guy she'd never met before?

What would she have said of Diane? How would she

have interpreted the events leading up to that final night?
Would she have seen something that he'd not seen until it
was too late?

CHAPTER TEN

BEFORE Abby opened her eyes she knew she was alone. Not that she'd expected anything else, but disappointment flooded through her nonetheless, tarnishing the afterglow.

As she shifted muscles she hadn't used in a long while made their presence felt, bringing back last night's images and sensations. The hairy masculine texture of Zak's skin rubbing against hers, his wickedly clever hands and mouth. The feel of him, hard, hot steel as he came in her hands.

But as she opened her eyes all she saw through the mosquito netting that Zak must have closed around her was the aftermath. The rumpled sheets, her dress and panties a haphazard pile of green silk on the floor, her shoes by the door.

No Zak to cuddle up against and relive the night with. No lovers' intimacy and cosy morning love-in.

No lover, period.

Not even his underwear, which he'd discarded so carelessly, so easily, last night. No, he was a few metres away, behind the *closed* rattan door. And, technically, they weren't lovers in the fullest sense of the word.

Because he hadn't brought condoms with him.

He'd never intended making love with her.

And why would he? He'd come to the wedding alone. She wasn't his partner; it just turned out that way later.

She rubbed a hand over the dull ache in her chest. What was it about him that pulled her heartstrings? He was unlike any man she'd ever known, except for her foster-father, Bill. Both men were genuine, generous and caring, willing to trust a girl they didn't know and give her a chance.

Except, unlike Bill, Zak had erected a barrier around his heart. He didn't show his emotions, lose control.

'Oh, but you did,' she said, her body tingling with remembered passion. He'd lost control—with her. For once he'd let go of that tension. Opened up. To her.

And tomorrow would they go back to business and pretend it never happened?

Hah. She shook her head as she swung her feet over the edge of the bed and padded naked to her bag. Only Zak could carry that off; she'd never look at Zak again and not remember what he looked like in the grip of passion. His gorgeous masculine body in full arousal, the sound of his deep-throated groan, the way he shuddered as he came.

Oh. My. Goodness. She blew out a heated breath as her hormones escalated again, speeding her pulse rate up.

Breakfast. Was it too early? she wondered, slipping on a floral sundress. She winced at the pain as she put on her sandals and slipped them off again. Quietly, so as not to disturb Zak—she did *not* want to face him yet—she opened her door to the moist tropical-scented air, and stepped into the morning. Away from the memories of last night.

It was still too early for most guests, but—*oh, no*—not for Zak, apparently, who had the buffet to himself. Abby almost turned back, but he caught sight of her and pulled out a chair.

'Good morning.' His eyes met hers and the air between them crackled.

'Good morning,' she said, as if she hadn't seen the raw passion in Zak's eyes as she'd opened herself to his gaze, his hands. His shattered control, her mindless moans…

'Juice?'

His voice dragged her attention back to the present and that same pair of eyes. 'Thanks.' She struggled for something to say. 'I'm feeling a little guilty that we didn't say goodbye to the newly-weds last night.'

'I said goodbye for both of us.'

'Oh?'

'I went back to the party…after.' He cleared his throat. 'I gave them your apologies. Said you had a headache.'

'You went back to the party?'

Why did she feel the sharp jab of disappointment? Because he hadn't cared enough to stay with her? Because it was only about sex for him?

So, okay, let it be just about sex. One night of amazing sex. They'd given each other mutual gratification. Even if they hadn't made it all the way.

Deliberately casual, she lifted her glass of juice, took a slow sip then said, 'I thought you were asleep—you seemed so relaxed.'

'I guess I wasn't as relaxed as I thought.'

Reaching for a slice of toast, she peeled open the little jam packet. 'So… What was last night? Do we call it a one-night stand?'

He blinked once, then his eyes narrowed. 'Abby, that's not how it is. Was.' For a long silent moment he said nothing as he stroked the moisture on the outside of his glass and pondered its contents. The same fingers that had stroked her body last night, the same eyes that had devoured every inch of her.

She had the feeling he was reliving it and trying to file it away in some neat little compartment in his mind. And perhaps he had, because he seemed to come to some grim conclusion.

The high she'd woken on deflated like a lead balloon. She felt it drop, felt her heart squeeze tight inside her chest.

'Abby,' he said slowly. 'Last night was good.' And the remnants blazed like blue flames in his eyes.

'Yes, it was good.' But it seemed fate didn't include a man who needed her, just her. Someone who wanted more than sex.

Then, damn him, he reached out, lay a hand on hers. One finger, to be precise. One sensory caress to send her nerve endings into a spin. Her gaze slid to their hands. That finger had touched her most intimate places last night and, oh, so skilfully.

'But I don't want a relationship right now,' he said. 'Better to know that up front. No one gets hurt.'

Too late.

'Excuse me.' She forced a smile that hardly touched her lips. 'I need…I need the bathroom. I'll be right back.'

She hurried to her hut, her eyes stinging with moisture, barely feeling the rough stones beneath her sore feet. She didn't need the bathroom. She needed a swim in the salt water to wash away the reminder of last night. Of losing him. She shook her head. She'd never really had him. In her room, she tossed off her sundress, pulled out her new black swimsuit and dragged it on. Slung her towel over her shoulder and grabbed her water bottle.

She followed the shoreline as it curved around a tiny inlet, lush foliage reaching almost to the water's edge. The sun was invisible, rising behind a bruised haze on the horizon, the water a flawless apricot mirror.

No more, she decided, and headed down to the harder sand. Dumped her towel. If Zak discovered how she felt about him—as a man, as a lover—she'd have to leave his home, leave Surfers. Find another town. She couldn't afford to start again, and she had to consider Aurora—she wanted her up here as soon as she could afford a place of her own, and that meant making Good Vibrations work.

Or had she ruined even that chance by becoming intimate with Zak last night?

A lump rose in her throat. What a mess she'd got herself into—falling for a man who didn't want a woman in his life. Not long-term anyway. Her toes curled at the lacy water's edge, as a storm of protest rose and blew right through her. No. *No, no, no.* Been there, done that. Past scars were imprinted on her heart and right now they were bleeding.

She dived in and started swimming.

Bracing his hands on his knees, Zak stopped running to catch his breath. And stared in horror as Abby plunged into the water. His pulse hammered in his ears till he was dizzy with it. Nausea prickled the back of his throat. 'Abby!'

He yanked off a sneaker as he ran to the water line. He should have known earlier that she didn't need the bathroom. He'd seen it in her eyes—the hurt, the sheen of tears. 'Stingers! In the water!'

She trod water to glance behind her, then, obviously not hearing his warning, turned away and began swimming straight out to sea. Away from him.

Diane all over again.

No! 'Stingers! Come out! Now!' He tried to yell, to shout, to warn her about the marine creatures that lurked in the shallows along the Queensland coast, but his throat was full of sawdust.

In his haste, he stumbled, dragged off his other sneaker, dropped it at the water's edge. Dragged his T-shirt over his head. Sweat broke out all over his body, his arms shook, his shuddering legs barely supported him. He hesitated only a second. Then the familiar sickening panic clawed up his throat as he plunged in after her.

He focused on regulating his erratic breathing, the rhythmic movement of his arms, the burn in his muscles, but the panic was alive inside him, a predator waiting to pounce the instant he gave in.

Finally his head popped up beside her. Relief swamped him. He grabbed her arm, squeezing so tight she winced, catching strands of her hair as he tugged her close. She was warm against the cool of the water, safe, in his arms, even if said arms were trembling like a newborn foal's legs.

'Stop it,' she shouted, thrashing her arms while he tried to hold her. 'What is your problem?'

Through sheer desperation he overpowered her attempts to wriggle out of his grasp. He had her, he wasn't letting her go. 'Stingers.' He swiped water from his eyes. 'Out, now.'

He saw fear widen her eyes and felt her resistance melt away. 'What? Oh, no! Zak!'

Their bodies bumped hard as he pulled her closer, then with the life-saving skills he'd learned years ago, he struck out for the shore with her in tow, long limbs tangling with his.

The instant they reached the shallows, he released her. He grabbed the nearest sneaker off the sand and walked jelly-kneed to where her belongings lay and faced away from her. He couldn't let her see him like this.

'Hey,' she said softly. 'I shouldn't have tried to push you away.' He heard her pick up her towel and rub it over her body. 'Thanks. I thought stingers were only around in sum—'

'And what the *hell* were you doing swimming alone?' Now they were safe, a dark tide of emotion surged and swamped him. He wanted to turn and shake the living daylights out of her. He wanted to plaster her against him and kiss her living, breathing body senseless.

'I didn't… What is it, Zak?'

Damn it. His vision turned grey, the sand spun up to meet him as he sank heavily to the ground. He propped his forearms on his raised knees and watched the water drip off his hair into the sand between his thighs. 'I'll be fine.'

'You're not fine now.' She moved in front of him, knelt and offered him the water bottle.

He tipped his head back and took a long swallow. Drew a deep unsteady breath. Avoided her eyes, which he knew were dark with concern. 'It's nothing.' With quick jerky movements, he grabbed his T-shirt, shoved his wet, sandy feet into his sneakers and started to push up.

But Abby was having none of it. She splayed her hand on his chest and held him there. 'I feel responsible. For heaven's sake, Zak. *Tell. Me.*'

'Water's not my thing, okay?' Disgusted with his weakness, he wrenched himself away from her touch and up.

'How can that be?' she said behind him. 'You swim like a professional.'

He closed his eyes, opened them again because all he could see was the black water beneath the bridge. 'My wife drowned after a car accident last year. I couldn't save her.'

Then he started walking.

* * *

Every organ, every limb in Abby's body turned to liquid as she watched him stride back the way he'd come, shoulders stiff, head bent. Her natural response was to go after him, but a deeper instinct rooted her to the spot. Go after him…to offer him…What? Comfort? Sympathy? An apology for behaving like a petulant child?

She hugged trembling arms around herself, chilled to the soul as his figure receded down the beach. No. The last thing he needed right now was her. In any way.

Wife.

Deceased wife.

Everything fell into place. It all made sickening sense. His problems with intimacy—which she'd all but taunted him about—his obsession with work, the haunted look she'd glimpse in his eyes after a sleepless night.

In heaven's name, why hadn't someone enlightened her? Why hadn't Zak just come out and told her right from the start? Was it so painful he couldn't bear to talk about it? The trauma of not being able to save her…

And she'd just reawakened those horrors by swimming away from him when she'd seen him on the beach.

She picked up her belongings and slowly made her way back along the sand. Obviously he was still mourning his wife. Last night…What had she done? What had *they* done? Because he'd been as willing as she. But *one night*, he'd said.

And that night was over.

When she reached her villa, she packed her stuff quickly and headed straight for the ablutions block. She stepped under the tepid spray. At least there was none of the shared-bathroom routine they'd become accustomed to. Rather than smooth tiles and the fragrance of Zak's toiletries, the experience was concrete floor and the smell of bleach.

Which served to highlight the urgency of finding her own place as soon as possible.

The sound of a chopper reached her ears as she exited. She was in time to see it put down on the helipad, saw Zak dump his belongings and climb in. She caught a glimpse of a gaunt face as he donned headphones, watched the chopper rise into the air and veer away.

Somehow Abby managed to get through the trip back, but she couldn't enjoy the luncheon on board or the beautiful tropical scenery they passed through. Just making conversation with virtual strangers was an effort. Thankfully Vince didn't come near her, otherwise occupied with the blonde she'd seen him with on the dance floor.

The minibus dropped her off at Capricorn Centre. She had no doubt he'd plunged himself into work already and they needed to talk about what had happened.

He wasn't there. The temp who was covering for Tina for the next couple of days told Abby Zak had taken four days' leave interstate on urgent family business.

Business? No way. That emotional island he'd exiled himself to was surrounded with cut glass rather than sand and, until he found his own way off it and was ready to talk, she had no way to reach him.

The indications were that Good Vibrations was going to be very successful if the volume of clientele that passed through Abby's door over the next two days was any indication. Her appointment book was full.

Her nights were lonely.

On the third morning Abby poked her head around Tina's office door. 'Hi, Mrs Langotti. Welcome back.'

The newly-wed woman looked up, the stars still in her eyes. 'Hi, Abby.'

'How was the honeymoon, as if I need to ask? That island is magic.'

'Only two days…and nights.' She grinned. 'Not long enough, but it was nice to come home to Danny.' Tina skirted her desk and came around to hug Abby, then leaned back to look at her. 'You and Zak seemed to be enjoying its magic, too— I couldn't help noticing.'

Abby's heart clenched. 'Oh, that…'

'And I think it's great,' Tina added. 'You're just what Zak needs right now.'

'Zak's not ready for a full-on relationship…'

'Abby. Honey.' Tina shook her head. 'From what I saw on the dance floor, he's well and truly ready. And about time, too.' She waved a well-manicured hand, her wedding ring glinting.

'I didn't know he'd been married.' She walked to the full-length window and breathed in the tropical scent outside. 'Why didn't you tell me, Tina?'

'I left that up to Zak,' she replied, her voice sobering.

'He took me into his home, gave me a place to set up my business. Did everything good and decent and honest. Except he left out that one very important detail.'

'And now everything's changed?' she heard Tina ask behind her.

Yeah. I love him.

Somehow those three little words slipped past her defences and rested like tears in her heart. *Forget falling, I'm in all the way over my head. In love with a man who's incapable of loving me back.*

'How did it happen?' Abby asked.

'Her car went over a bridge. Zak was following in his own car. He dived off the bridge but she was trapped inside.

There was nothing he could have done, but he jumped anyway. We almost lost him, too.'

'The scars on his thigh.'

'Yes. Diane was my best friend. The three of us grew up together. I miss her, too.'

'I'm sorry.'

'So are we all. I have a picture… I was going to put it on my desk… I just haven't got around to it.' Tina walked to a pile of boxes, rummaged a moment, then dusted off a framed photograph of Zak and Diane with her and Nick.

Abby couldn't take her eyes off Diane. She could have been a model or a movie star. Sleek and sophisticated, and that one dress would have cost more than Abby's annual income. Both she and Zak looked every bit the successful cosmopolitan couple that graced the front pages of women's magazines.

'I'm sorry, Tina.' She reached for her hand. 'I wish he'd told me.' *I've made such a fool of myself.*

Back in her shop, Abby blended her oils of cedar wood, jasmine and ylang-ylang and set them in the vaporiser, but instead of focusing on her next client all she could see was Diane's face.

How much Zak must have loved her to risk his life in such a hazardous attempt. Had Diane known how much? Had she appreciated what a diamond of a man she'd married? Of course—they'd been a part of each other's lives since childhood. A love that had lasted decades; it was no wonder he'd exiled himself to shut out the emotional pain. No wonder he never wanted to love again. He might want Abby in a physical way, but that was where it ended.

He was still in love with his wife.

CHAPTER ELEVEN

ZAK buckled into his business-class seat for the flight home, breathing a sigh as he watched Sydney's distinctive skyline of Bridge and Opera House disappear beneath low cloud.

His family had been surprised to see him, especially grubby and dishevelled after two days camping out in the bush. He'd used those two days to come to an important decision. Then he'd called them together to explain why he was selling Forrester Building Restorations.

'A drink from the bar, sir?' asked the flight attendant, already pulling down his tray.

'Bourbon on ice, thanks.' He didn't normally drink before noon but today he had to talk to Abby. The prospect scared him almost as much as his quick and shocking dip in the sea. She deserved so much more than he'd given her and somehow he was going to make it up to her in every way possible, if she'd let him.

He loved her.

The acknowledgement might be four days young, and several weeks late, but it still had the power to grab him by the throat, a surge of emotion that had him clenching his hands around his drink and leaning back breathless in his seat.

But it had taken that moment on the island to realise his guilt over Diane's death was nothing compared to the thought of losing Abby. His life was empty without her.

He missed her sunny laugh, that way she had of lifting her shoulder when she talked. She could raise his spirits with just a look, a touch, a word, even when he did his damnedest to ignore her. He loved her positive outlook on life, never questioning the way he chose to live his.

Except to coax him out of his shell. Which, on reflection, was what he'd needed. She'd turned his life around. Had him looking at things he'd not seen before.

Abigail Seymour, who was all wrong for him, had somehow slipped past his defences.

His hand tightened around his glass as he gazed out at the cotton-wool clouds that stretched on for ever. Diane was gone. He'd loved her, but he'd lost her before she'd driven that car over the bridge. Finally, the truth he'd been too stubborn, too hurt, to admit.

He hadn't neglected his wife; they'd grown apart with the years, both busy with their respective careers. But Diane *had* been different those last months. Unhappy. She'd been drunk when she'd got behind the wheel of her car that night. He'd never forgiven himself for not being close enough to snatch the keys from her hand and stop her leaving.

Was he going to continue to punish himself for that for the rest of his life? Or was he going to start again with a new foundation and build something worthwhile? With Abby.

The knowledge he'd imprisoned ruthlessly behind bars of denial burst free. His heart pounded in his chest and crawled up his throat. Every part of his body flexed and tingled. It was like waking up after a coma—and he knew, all too well, how that felt.

Don't give up on me just yet, baby, he willed her silently.

As soon as the plane touched down at the Gold Coast airport, he picked up his car and went straight to Capricorn Centre. He was still figuring the best way to go about it. He knew he had some explaining to do. Knew Abby would be hurt, probably angry. He hoped what he had to say would change that.

Perhaps a late lunch or early dinner? A stroll along the beach that she loved so much? Then he glanced at the thunderheads building over the sea. Not a walk, then.

'It's her afternoon off,' the hairdresser in the shop next to Abby's told him when he found her door closed. 'She said she was going apartment hunting.'

The information drove a fist square into his solar plexus, knocking the breath from his body and souring the anticipation of seeing her.

It rolled around in his gut like a lead ball all the way home. Why was she rushing into something she obviously knew sweet nothing about? With her track record, he didn't trust her not to get tangled up in some dodgy contract.

His hand rasped across the stubble of his three-day-old beard. He knew why.

He swung into the drive a tad too fast, skidded to a halt at the base of the front stairs rather than detour round the back. Meanwhile, he needed a shower, a shave and a cold beer. He could manage two out of three at the same time.

Thunder rumbled in the distance as he tossed his bag on the bed, stripped down to his skin and turned the ceiling fan on full-blast to cool the sweat of the afternoon on his skin. Went to the kitchen, popped the top on a can, then padded back to the bedroom.

He opened the *en suite* door and took two steps in before he realised the air was filled with fragrant steam—*feminine* fragrant steam—and he wasn't alone.

Abby. On hands and knees scrubbing his shower tiles. Wearing nothing but a doll-sized white thong and a low-cut bra. Leaving her all-but-exposed bottom wiggling in time with music only she could hear through the MP3 player dangling round her neck.

His eyes took all that in for a stunned ten seconds while every muscle in his body locked down. While the blood drained from his head and rushed to another part of his anatomy. Another rapidly growing *exposed* part of his anatomy.

This wasn't the way he'd planned it.

Backtrack before she sees you. The order didn't quite reach his feet before she straightened to reclip the wayward hair escaping from its clasp on top of her head. She must have caught some subtle movement or felt the heat of his presence because her head snapped around. A startled gasp and it was too late.

Her eyes flared in panic, then she mouthed his name around an O of surprise, and that panicked gaze calmed a little, turning wary but aware as her eyes flicked down, then back to his face.

Damn. 'Why in heaven's name are you cleaning in here at this time of day?' he demanded, his breath whistling out between his teeth. 'You know I don't expect you to clean up after me.' Beer sloshed over his hand as he set the can on the vanity.

'What?' She tugged out the earplugs. He heard the MP3 slide onto the tiles with a soft metallic clink as she scrambled up. 'I didn't expect you…' she rushed on before he could repeat his question. She looked to the damp towel she'd left on the vanity, but he needed it more than she did.

He stayed where he was, reached out and slung it around his hips. But the damage was done. He forced himself to speak slowly, calmly over the gravel in his throat. 'What's wrong with the other bathroom?'

'Nothing. It's so much easier to clean the shower straight after you've used it and since I'd left my shower gel in here…'

Her voice trailed off—at least he thought it did because he stopped listening. Her freshly showered skin was a delicate shade of coral pink. Except for dusky rose nipples that puckered beneath the sheer fabric of her bra even as he tried not to notice.

It took another thick and heavy beat that pulsed in the steamy air and echoed low in his body to realise he wasn't the only one *not* noticing.

'I'll just—'

'Tess told me you were apartment hunting.' He couldn't help that it sounded like an accusation. And why the blazes were they holding a conversation as if they were passing the time of day on the back veranda?

Her eyes jerked back to his and something flickered in their depths that scared the living daylights out of him. 'I did… I was… I finished. Zak…' A soft feminine sound erupted from her throat. 'This is awkward.'

He remained rooted to the spot. Had she found somewhere else? His heart thundered like the approaching storm. Something like pain tightened his jaw, had his hands curling into fists. He wouldn't ask her about that now.

'I'm sorry,' she whispered. 'I'll get out of your way.'

His stomach muscles bunched as he sucked in a breath,

his groin heating, hardening to the point of pain as she took the necessary steps towards him to reach the door and escape.

The scent of her body, its cool satin smoothness as her arm brushed his, snatched away reason and snapped his tenuous hold on control.

'Don't go.' He heard the rawness in his voice as he turned into her closeness on a soft oath, curling his hands around her upper arms and spinning her to face him. He slammed his mouth down on hers before she could respond. The primitive hunger beat in his blood as he dragged her flush against him until her mouth opened beneath his.

He drank in the dark honeyed taste like a dying man—its sweetness, its promise. He wanted her with tongue and lips and hands, from her mouth to her toes and every place between.

And he wanted it now.

He rushed his hands over the taut, firm lines of her body, sprang open her bra clasp and groaned as he filled his palms with her flesh, her nipples hard against his chest. Not enough.

With his mouth still fused to hers, grasping her buttocks, he swung her around and set her on the vanity. Watched her eyes darken as he spread her legs wide, saw his own eyes glaze over in the mirror's reflection above her head. His arm knocked his beer can; it tipped and rolled, spilling amber liquid over the counter and onto the floor.

Her hips were curved, cool, taut. The inside of her thighs were smooth, deliciously hot. When he ran his knuckles over the tiny triangle of fabric he found it damp and steamy with desire. His knees turned weak, his vision hazed, but he saw her eyes erupt like silver lava and fuse with his.

Watching him, she took the clasp from her hair, freeing her auburn curls, a riot of red streaming over her shoulders. Then, leaning back on her palms, she arched her hips, offering herself to him.

The only answer he needed.

Snap. One firm tug on the strap at her side and her thong was history. He shoved it to one side, pulled her forward until she teetered on the edge of the vanity and set his mouth on the soft skin of her neck.

Sweet, everywhere sweet. He moved lower, over the erotic ridge of collarbone, nuzzling, tasting, teeth and tongue scraping over her flesh while her fingers twined in his hair and tugged on his ears. Her heart beat a fast and frantic rhythm against his hand when he kneaded her breasts.

Lower. At last he was where he wanted to be—close to her heart. Taking one pebble-hard nipple into his mouth, he suckled her, drawing it out with his teeth while he pinched the other between finger and thumb, rolled his hand over it to feel its hardness against his tingling palm.

No thought, just aching, endless need.

'Yes,' she moaned, a strangled sound at the first touch of his fingers on her woman's flesh. Where he burned to touch her again.

Her breath puffed in short serrated gasps against his ear as he plunged his fingers into her wetness and heat, drawing the dewy moisture out and over, up and over until she bucked against him and cried out his name.

His name. Possessiveness lanced through him like a flaming arrow.

A flash of lightning freeze-framed the abandon on her face, an earthy enchantress bathed in silver as she threw her head back, her hair spiralling out of control in the moist air, fingernails digging half-moons in his shoulders while the thunder rumbled nearer.

Alive, so alive. Impossibly high, as if she soared on the wings of angels. The world was still spinning when Abby blinked the haze from her eyes to focus on the wild-eyed, hungry male in front of her. 'Zak.' Her voice sounded hoarse, not like hers at all. 'Please…say…you have condoms…'

'In here.' His breath came out harsh, his eyes never left her face as he tugged open the vanity drawer. He pulled out an unopened packet.

'Hurry.' Her heart seemed to grow too big for her chest, her blood speeding too fast through her veins as he fought the packaging with clumsy fingers.

'Quick.' Finally. She held her breath as he ripped the foil open. 'Now, Zak.' *Before you think about it.*

Before I can think that this is a bad idea.

Almost before he'd finished protecting himself she shimmied forward, wrapped her legs around him, dragging him closer, catching his face between her hands until all she could see was the laser-blue intensity of his eyes.

Hers. Just for this moment he was utterly hers.

No patience for either of them, just need, frantic and fevered. And, oh, he was so hot, so huge, so hungry as he pushed inside her, ruthlessly filling her with his steel-hard strength, learning the most intimate secrets of her body as she learned his.

It was like the storm, all sparks and noise and energy. A cacophony of sensations battering her as she matched her pace to his. Heat where his body drove into hers, where chest abraded breasts. Power in the arms that bound her against him like chains.

His demand, its dark turbulence, pounded her, swept her up again, lifting her higher, higher, and she grabbed hold of his neck and bit his shoulder, afraid she might spin off the face of the earth. 'Hold me.' She almost sobbed. 'Don't let me go.'

'I've got you, baby.'

The thread of gentleness in his harsh tone undid her, but he drove into her until there wasn't room for reason or thought or breath. Until passion exploded and consumed her whole.

She remembered collapsing against him, his sweat-covered chest against her cheek as he lifted her and carried her to his bed. Rain falling, its green drift of scent over cooling skin. His heart beating heavy beneath her ear as he tucked her head against his armpit.

Thundery late afternoon sun filled the room with a murky orange glow. Abby lay skin to sticky skin with a hot-bodied Zak. Her mind was mud. What had just happened? A few moments later, she rose carefully on one elbow to watch him. His eyes were closed, and for once in his life his body looked relaxed.

Her chest both tightened and expanded with love. Oh, this was a heartbreak in waiting. She let her gaze roam over his naked body. Long, lean and hard with a dusting of dark masculine hair that arrowed down to…a very impressive package. His legs were entwined with hers, the skin dark gold against her fair ones.

But it was his face that drew her. She'd see that face in her dreams as long as she lived. His eyes, a burning blue in the throes of passion. Eyes that could turn as remote as a New Zealand glacier, or as mysterious as the deepest ocean with one blink.

And now she knew why. A secret that, for reasons of his own, he'd chosen not to share with her.

She didn't want to disturb him quite yet. She needed another moment to watch him.

She'd seen Diane's photo; she knew Abby with the frizzy hair and freckles would never fit into his life. Nor would she change the woman she was, for anyone. She was comfortable with who she was. That didn't alter the fact that she loved him—for who *he* was. Very slowly she freed her legs from his.

'Where're you going?' a sleepy voice drawled, the sound sliding over her like dark chocolate. He rolled over, and, with one large calloused hand beneath her breasts, scooted her close so that he lay hot—and already hard again—against her. Temptation never sounded so good. Never felt so good.

No, no, no. Abby extricated herself, her skin gliding over the expensive cotton sheets as she moved to the edge of the mattress and sat up. There were three people in this bed. 'You need that shower now,' she said. 'I'll be in the kitchen when you're ready to talk.'

So hard to leave his room naked, knowing he tracked her every step to the door, to escape to her own room and drag on shorts and top with trembling fingers. To tame the nest of hair the steam—and Zak—had rendered feral. And try very very hard not to cry.

She heard his shower running and chopped salad vegetables for something to do with her hands while she waited.

His eyes clashed with hers the moment he entered the kitchen, but they held firm, unwilling to let her go, and for a moment she was spellbound, her whole body aching and tense, remembering how those eyes had burned with passion not thirty minutes ago.

They burned now, but with a different emotion. Did she see regret or self-recrimination in their depths? Hell, she couldn't read him with her own emotions churning inside her like a blender.

He was wearing jeans and his navy knit shirt. His hair was damp and the thick stubble that had felt so good against her face and breasts was gone.

The knife she was gripping skated off the carrot and skidded over her finger. Damn! She walked to the sink and wrenched on the tap as blood welled over her fingers.

'Let me look at that,' he said, behind her.

'It's only a scratch. All it needs is a Band-Aid.' Shrugging him off, she moved to a nearby cupboard and reached for the packet in the first-aid box. She sealed the dressing, flexed her finger. If only emotions could be mended as easily.

'Stop it,' he said, and took the knife from her hand, set it on the bench with a clatter. 'I'm sorry.' He gripped her chin, forced her to look at him. 'I should've told you.'

'Yes, you should have. Why didn't you? You must have known how I felt about you.'

Acknowledgement burned in his gaze. 'I didn't want to see the sympathy—not in your eyes, Abby. I've had a gutful of sympathy over the past year. No more.'

'Not sympathy. Understanding.'

'I don't want that either, because no one really understands.'

'Okay. Help me understand. Tell me about Diane.'

He rubbed his chest, as if to ease an ache. 'What do you want to know?'

Everything. Nothing. Did you love her? Stupid question. Stick to the mundane. 'Was she involved in your business, too?'

'No.'

Something in his voice prompted Abby to say, 'I'm not the only one who thought you worked too hard, then. Did she work?'

'She was a fashion buyer for a department-store chain.'

'So…she travelled?'

'Sydney, Melbourne. The occasional trip to Asia.'

'She went alone?'

One hand fisted on the counter-top. 'I had the business.'

Ah.

'The night she died, I accused her of having an affair,' he said, and the fist curled tighter. 'I'll never know if that was true or not. She died before we could thrash it out.'

The information was a surprise to Abby. Yet…on reflection, perhaps not. 'You blame yourself.'

He let out a slow sigh and his whole body seemed to implode.

'How long are you going to hold onto that guilt, Zak? Because until you free yourself you'll never move on. You're not ready for a new relationship. You've demonstrated that over and over. Have you forgotten that only a few days ago you told me you're not looking for a relationship?'

His jaw clenched, and something flickered in his eyes. 'That was before—'

'You went AWOL for four days,' she interrupted. 'Not a word from you, Zak. I only found out when the temp at Capricorn Centre told me. Is that the sign of a healthy relationship? If what we have can even be termed a relationship.'

And because she didn't want to hear excuses, even legitimate ones, she picked up the knife again, and tapped it firmly on the counter. Looked into the eyes of the man who'd held her body and her heart in his hands and steeled herself. 'You know how I feel about you, but I'm through with the emotional merry-go-round.'

He shook his head. 'Damn it, Abby,' he said softly. 'Don't give up on me now.'

God knew she didn't want to, but could she trust him not to reject her again? 'We need some space. Which is handy because I arranged to go over to Tina's tonight. I can't cancel now. Nick's gone to Brisbane and in return for a traditional roast-lamb dinner I'm giving her a massage— if Daniel allows it. And since I'm in the mood to drink to excess tonight I promised to sleep over.'

'I can pick you up.'

'No,' she said firmly. 'I need this for me. Use the time to catch up on work. Your businesses must be falling apart without you.' She heard the sarcasm in her voice and wasn't sorry for it.

'I'm selling Forrester Building Restorations. Already have some interested parties.'

A glimmer of hope lit inside Abby. 'Well, that's…a start.' She nodded. 'That's good. But how does your dad feel about it?'

'I flew down to Sydney, talked to Dad and the rest of the family. They understand, and they're okay with it.'

'Great. I hope it works out for you.' And before she could change her mind, she slipped past him and headed for her room to pack her overnight gear.

He was already gone before she left.

CHAPTER TWELVE

AT CAPRICORN CENTRE Zak shut down his computer at 2:00 a.m. Because he'd seen the determination in Abby's eyes, because she'd already made plans and he had no right to make demands after pulling his own disappearing act, he'd used the evening as she'd suggested, but he hadn't achieved much. He closed his door, and instead of heading out he found himself walking down the now-empty corridor to Abby's shop.

Using his master key, he let himself inside. Light from the lobby filtered through the large shop window so he left the shop's lighting off. The cool air that greeted his nostrils was tinged with the fragrance of the essences she used, the ones he smelled on her when they were in the same room at home.

He ran his fingers through the dish of tumbled crystals she kept by the cash register, listening to the clacking sound they made and feeling their smooth surfaces against his skin. What would she say if he booked himself in for that promised massage? The scenario of him lying on her massage mat and letting her fingers work his stiff neck muscles skated through his veins like quicksilver. He flicked through her appointment book and saw tomorrow's schedule was full.

His gaze snagged on the hat-stand and the white jersey leggings and top she wore while working. He couldn't help himself. He walked over to feel its texture and breathe in that familiar scent some more.

He wanted to be with her again. Connected. The way they'd been together this afternoon.

The house was dark when he pulled up ten minutes later, another reminder that Abby wasn't there—no porch light illuminated his way.

He walked down the hall to his room, but paused at her door. It was open, the curtains drawn back. 'Abby,' he murmured into the darkness, his pulse gearing up in hopeful anticipation of touching his mouth to her sleep-soft lips even though he knew she wasn't there.

He waded through the semi-darkness to her bed. His hand slid over the quilt. No warm bumps, the way it should feel with a curvaceous body beneath it. He could still smell her fragrance mingled with sunshine-fresh linen.

'Come back,' he said into the silence.

He walked on to his own room. The sheets were still rumpled from their afternoon. Then he saw the note on the pillow.

Dear Zak,
I hope you didn't work too late. Get some sleep tonight and I'll see you at work. A. X

He glared at her trademark flamboyant A and that simple kiss. He wanted that kiss delivered in person.

His hand halted midway through his furrowed hair. A gem of an idea glimmered in his mind. He flipped open his planner, checked some numbers and started making a list.

* * *

'Can't sleep?'

Abby turned, her teacup in her hand rather than the alcohol she'd promised herself. A sleep-deprived Tina was jostling a fussy Daniel on her hip. At least they'd squeezed in a massage before he'd woken up.

'Not yet. I just made some valerian tea and honey. Want some?'

Tina's nose wrinkled as she reached for a baby bottle she'd prepared earlier. 'I'll pass, thanks, although perhaps I should put some in Danny's bottle; give us both some peace.'

'Let me take him for a few moments.' Setting her cup on the table, she clapped her hands and reached for the child. 'Come to Auntie Abby?' Sucking on two fingers, Danny regarded her with wide dark eyes.

'That'd be great, I need to go to the bathroom. Won't be a minute.' And without waiting for his lordship's approval, Tina delivered Danny into Abby's arms.

'Take your time.' Maternal instincts Abby didn't know she had swirled to life inside her at the contact of petal-soft flesh against hers. 'Hello, sweetie, you giving your mummy a hard time?' Abby cuddled the restless child, rubbed her cheek over the soft fuzzy head, inhaling his sweet baby-powder scent. 'You know, I don't get the opportunity to do this very often,' she told him softly.

For a dreamy moment, as she rocked from side to side, she was immersed in a daydream of holding her own child. A little boy with blue eyes like his dad and the cutest dimples you ever saw. Her womb tightened at the image, and she shivered.

'I've got him,' she told Tina when she returned, unwilling to give him up just yet. 'I think he's settling.'

Tina smiled. 'Another first. At night he usually turns

into a real mummy's boy.' She sat down at the table and watched Abby. 'Motherhood would look good on you.'

'Only in a safe and secure marriage, thanks.'

'No marriage is totally safe and secure,' Tina said.

Abby knew Tina was thinking of Diane. How even the happiest marriage could be over in the blink of an eye. Abby was thinking of her own mother and Hayley and the tough times they'd lived through.

She touched her lips to Danny's head. 'That makes it all the more important to cherish what you have while you can.'

'Speaking of which, I wonder whether Zak's still burning the midnight oil.'

Abby beat back the image of Zak burning the midnight oil with her not so many nights ago. 'It's not that serious between us, Tina.'

Tina cocked her head. 'You try looking in the mirror and telling yourself that, girl, because I see a different view from this side.'

Abby sighed. 'Until Zak's over Diane…'

'He needs a gentle push, or even a shove, and you're the one to give it to him. I saw the way he watched you at the wedding. And I know it wasn't a headache you had on our wedding night.' She leaned back in her chair. 'So what's your next move?'

Abby shook her head. 'The next move is his.'

Zak missed her arrival the following morning, but he knew Abby was already in the building because he'd smelled her perfume waft past his door while he was on a conference call.

The instant he put down the phone, he left his office and headed for Good Vibrations. She'd already changed into that sexy white uniform that moulded to her shape—he could see the generous globes of her breasts and the distinct jut of her nipples against the fabric.

At the moment she was mixing a potpourri of scented oils. Mood music, which reminded him of a tranquil lake, played softly in the background.

She looked up when she saw him, her smile clouding a smidgen as she poured the oil into a vaporiser and lit the candle. 'Good morning, Mr Forrester.'

'I'm glad you think so. What—?'

'I'll be right with you, Mrs Dexter,' she called, jerking her head towards the screen behind her and spoke softly. 'You'll scare your guests away. I can't talk now, I have a client.'

He grasped her forearm, registered the familiar contours of bone and flesh, of heat and strength. Looked into those clear grey eyes that told him sweet nothing about what she was thinking. But he lowered his voice. 'When are you free?'

She slipped out of his grasp, only because he let her go. 'I'm booked right through today.'

Of course, he already knew that. 'Lunch—'

'Sorry, meeting with a sales rep about some coloured essences I'm interested in trialling. I plan to eat here while she talks.'

He snapped his palms firmly on the counter, squared his gaze, spoke through his teeth so only she could hear. 'Make time for me.'

He saw the tiny flinch as she set her own jaw. 'Okay…' She reached for a pen. 'Since you're the boss.' Her eyes flashed up at him, then she made a formal note in her planner. *Zak Forrester.* 'Your appointment's for six-thirty.'

Patience was not his strong suit, but he'd take what he could get. He nodded. 'I'll meet you here. Six-thirty.'

* * *

At six twenty-five, he shut down his computer. At six twenty-seven Tina poked her head in the doorway as he was packing his briefcase. 'Zak, can you sign some cheques before you go?'

He checked his watch. 'Leave them on my desk. I'll do it in the morning.'

'I really need them signed now, if you wouldn't mind. I have to—'

'Okay, okay. Where are they?'

'In my office.'

He closed his eyes briefly and prayed for restraint. 'Right behind you.' Why in heaven's name couldn't she have brought them with her?

He cast only a cursory glance as he scrawled his signature on the line. 'Have a good evening, Tina.'

By the time he made it to Good Vibrations it was six thirty-three and her door was shut.

As his fist curled in frustration against the glass panel the door slid open a fraction. As he tapped lightly to alert her to his presence he caught a glimmer of something. A flicker of light, on the ceiling behind the privacy screen where Abby did her massage.

He stepped inside, cleared his throat, watching the flicker on the ceiling blossom into a glow, dancing as a distorted shadow formed, grew and receded. 'I can come back if you're still busy,' he called.

'No, I'm ready for you.'

Her words, spoken in that low, melodic voice, were like a torch to dry grass. But as she appeared from behind the screen Abby in work-mode was a different woman from the one he knew—or thought he knew. Still in her whites, she looked as fresh as she would at 9:00 a.m. The exuberance was still there, but hidden behind a professional demeanour.

'Hi, Zak. Come on in.'

She stepped behind him and closed the door. The air eddied around her, a mix of musky feminine sweat and the exotic fragrances he'd come to associate with her.

He heard the lock click and his pulse spiked. But he stayed where he was—in unfamiliar territory. An empty shop bore no resemblance to this intimate room with its Bolivian lounge music and candles that spread shadows and smelled like orange blossoms.

'How's your day been?' she asked, a hand lifted, indicating he should precede her to the other side of the screen. Pleasant and polite, the way she'd ask any client.

'Good, busy. Abby—' He made a move towards her but she sidestepped out of his reach and rounded the screen.

'Come on through. I'm just warming the oil.'

'Oil?'

'For your massage. It's a blend of lavender, orange and sandalwood—good for insomnia.'

'We need to clear up a few things.' He came to an abrupt halt at the foot of her massage mat. 'That's why I'm here.' His gaze took in the scene. A dozen scented candles— violet, a couple of pink, a red. The sound of water trickled over the tabletop fountain in the corner. 'I'm not one of your clients.'

'You asked, *demanded*—' she sweetened the word with a quick smile as she took a folded towel from her stack '—me to make a time for you.'

'Not an appointment.'

She smiled again. 'It's on the house. I promised you a massage, remember?'

Vividly.

That same hot, needy tension knotted at the base of his spine and worked its way up, only now it was tangled with other, more volatile and deeper emotions he struggled to control.

'I'll wait out front while you remove your clothing,' she said. 'You can leave your underwear on. Lie on your stomach and cover yourself with this.' She handed him the towel, then moved to the screen. 'Let me know when you're ready. Zak. Trust me, you'll enjoy it and it'll help you sleep tonight.'

He pierced her with a telling look. 'What if I don't want to sleep tonight?'

He saw something infinitely sad cloud her eyes that cooled his blood a few degrees and put his hormones on hold. 'Tonight's not about seduction,' she said. 'And it's not about sex.'

While he tried to come to terms with that plainly stated fact, she waited, her arms crossed beneath her breasts. 'I want to give you something back. I *need* to give you something back. Can you understand that?'

And in a sudden flash of insight, he grasped her meaning, understood that need. Give and take. Sometimes you had to take from someone, accept their gift, in order to give. He'd never allowed Abby that self-satisfaction or given her that validation.

He would have spoken but his throat was clogged with emotion, so he nodded and slipped open the first button of his shirt.

Drawing a breath as soon as he was alone, he tossed his clothes on a stool, lay on the mat as instructed and closed his eyes. At his muttered 'ready,' she returned.

She adjusted the towel over his body and he heard her rubbing oil into the palms of her hands as she knelt at the crown of his head. The heat from her body carried her scent with it, reminding him of the last time she'd been this close… *Tonight's not about sex.* He repeated the mantra as she leaned over him. If he opened his eyes… No.

With the first warm glide of her hands over his back, he tensed, the pressure in his groin skyrocketing. This was never going to work. 'I don't—'

But she placed one soothing, almost impersonal hand on the base of his spine, the other at his neck. 'Draw in the breath slowly, imagine a peach-coloured mist. Think of some place peaceful.' Then she continued with long, slow sweeps up the spine, around his ribcage, over his shoulders.

Not about sex. Not about sex. He slowly relaxed as the comforting warmth seeped through skin and muscle as she worked over his back, drawing away the tension, easing him into a state of semi-bliss, semi-sleep, semi-arousal.

She worked with skill. Magic. Whether her fingers were being playful, passionate or professional he could honestly say no one had ever touched him the way Abby did. She was the most giving person he'd ever met. She understood him better than anyone.

And he'd pushed her away too many times.

Abby felt him tense just then and wondered what he thought of, but kept her mind focused on the task and her strokes smooth, applying more pressure to the knots of tension in his shoulders. Refusing to think about the last time she'd touched him and how he'd taste if she leaned down.

The healing energy in her hands burned and tingled as she worked around the ugly scar tissue that puckered his left buttock, reminding her of what he'd risked to earn it and why.

She ended with a deep massage to his thighs, worked her way to his feet. Finally, she closed her eyes, drew her hands slowly up his spine, wrapping him in a healing pink mist. As she replaced the towel over his body, and pulled back to rest her bottom on her heels, she offered up a silent prayer of thanks that she'd had him in her life, even if it was for a short time.

'I want you in my life, Abigail Seymour.'

The softly slurred words pierced her soul. She wanted that, too. She wanted it all—his name, his love, his babies. But she couldn't be with that man until he came to terms with his loss and made changes.

She lay a light hand on his back, to simply feel him. 'Lie a moment, let your body come to slowly.'

He rolled over, dragging the towel with him. 'You've changed me. You're one of a kind, Abby, and very special. So special I—'

'If you're happy with the changes, then I've done my job.' She pushed up on unsteady legs, moved to the tiny basin and washed the feel of his skin, his scent, from her hands.

He sat up. His blue eyes captured hers, dark with old emotion.

And Abby's heart plunged into those murky depths with his. She wanted to kneel down beside him, to touch him again, as a therapist or a friend. But if she touched him now she might never let go. 'You came to talk. So talk.'

He heaved a big sigh and seemed resigned. 'You were right yesterday. I blame myself. I didn't take the time to find out what was bothering Diane.' His hand rasped over his evening stubble and his gaze lingered on a candle's flickering flame. 'If I hadn't known she was drunk, if I hadn't followed her to make sure she didn't get herself in trouble, she might not have skidded off that bridge.'

'No, but she might have killed someone else, as well as herself.'

His gaze swung back to her. It seemed to absorb her inside him, as if she had no will of her own. 'I'm through with the guilt trip, Abby. I just want to get on with my life.'

And he wanted her in it? No mention of love and ever after. So he wanted her for what? Sex? Friendship? *Not enough. Not nearly enough.* She tore her eyes away. She couldn't be only a friend to Zak any more. She loved him but until he felt the same way…

She wiped her hands, flung the towel over the basin and hugged her arms. 'You have your conference centre, and I have to concentrate on Good Vibrations and bringing Aurora here.' She switched on the main light and blew out the candles; so not the way to end a session. But then, she hadn't thought about that.

She'd come in early tomorrow and clean up—for two reasons. One: if she stayed a minute longer she'd lose it and she was *not* going to cry in front of him. Reason number two: if she left now, she could be out of the car park and away before he'd finished dressing. He wouldn't dare leave the centre in nothing but a towel. 'Close up when you're done, will you?' she said, and headed for the door.

'Wait. We're not finished.'

Behind the screen she heard a thump and the sound of clothes being tossed about. Grabbing her purse, she whisked out of the door with a quick, 'See you in the morning.'

She was wrong. As she pulled out of her parking spot she caught sight of a bare-chested Zak in her rear-vision mirror, trousers low on his hips, half running, half stumbling barefoot across the car park.

CHAPTER THIRTEEN

ABBY lay in her moon-drenched room, gazing up at the ceiling. The evening songs of insects filled the air. Pushing the sheet away, she closed her eyes and willed herself to sleep. Impossible.

There was an ache in her heart that no amount of sleep medication could dull. She wanted Zak in her life. He'd told her the same thing. Why couldn't it be that simple? An extended fling—wouldn't that work? Until they called it a day. Correction: until Zak called it a day. And, no, it wouldn't work, because for her love was for keeps. Good with the bad.

'You know I could have you evicted for unprofessional conduct. Leaving a client dangling…'

Abby's eyes slammed open at the sound of Zak's voice. He closed the door quietly behind him. He was still bare-chested, his bare feet soundless on the polished boards as he crossed the room. At least she imagined they were soundless because all she could hear was the boom of her suddenly wildly out-of-control heart beating in her ears.

His face was in silhouette, except for the glinting eyes, which held a hint of jest beneath the gravity. Moonlight painted silver over the hard planes and angles of the rest of him, inky black flowed into the little dip that was his navel. He looked like a superhero from some future world. A superhero with a sense of humour.

'You weren't exactly *dangling*.' And despite her inner turmoil she couldn't help a grin. 'Isn't there something in your employees' handbook about a dress code? The manager seen running through the centre half naked…'

'You. You make me do things I'd never do under normal circumstances.' He shook his head. 'Okay, I think we're even.' He sat down beside her on the bed, his face coming into view as the moonlight struck it. His palm cupped her face, warm and calloused, his eyes filled with promised pleasures. 'Come to my room.'

The smile hovering on her lips faded as her heart clenched. 'No, Zak.'

'Suit yourself, then, but it'll be a little crowded.'

Still sitting on the bed, he unzipped his trousers, shoved them down with his boxers and stretched out beside her.

She didn't argue. Couldn't seem to get her voice to work, to tell him to go. The hard strength of his thigh abraded her sensitive inner skin as he tangled it with hers, his hand searing her belly through her oversize T-shirt. Could he hear her heart thudding against his as she could hear his against her own?

'Abby,' he murmured.

Then his lips slid over hers and settled and she melted into him with a murmur of surrender. Just this once. One more time to sip at the taste of his lips, to explore the velvet of his mouth and swirl her tongue over his. One more chance to feel the weight of his body covering hers and listen to his voice hoarse with passion against her ear.

His hand found the hem of her T-shirt and glided beneath it; hot fingers seeking out her nipple, rolling, pinching, squeezing. Gently, so gently. Then up, taking the fabric with him so that he could lay his lips and tongue on the aching points he'd aroused while his hand slid along the underside of her upper arm, pushing it up and over her head.

She arched a foot, slid it along his calf to feel the texture of hairy skin against her sensitive sole. Tilted her pelvis and rubbed up against the hard, hot ridge of silken steel between them. Moisture formed a delicious friction, and she reached down to touch him there, her fingers reacquainting themselves with his shape and size.

Zak rocked against her, loving the way she stroked him, her little noises of approval and enjoyment. So responsive, so willing. He had to keep her in his life; he wanted her more than he'd wanted anything. He needed her more than his next breath. Couldn't she see that?

He leaned up on his arms to look down on her. Moonlight threaded through her hair, glistened like tiny diamonds on her dewy skin. He trailed one hand from the ridge of collarbone, over a breast, the curve of her waist, till he covered her fingers with his.

Leaning over the side of the bed, he grabbed his trousers and withdrew a condom from his pocket. She nodded, her pewter eyes turning slumberous as he slid the protection on. Then he pushed inside slowly, drawing out the sensations—smooth and tight and hot—every centimetre pure pleasure.

She moaned and writhed beneath him and the sound of her passion was the sweetest music he'd ever heard. He didn't need her words, didn't offer any. Hands that had massaged him with such skill earlier turned intimate, tensing and flexing and slipping over his back in a sinuous rhythm that echoed his movements.

They moved in sync, fitted together as if they'd been constructed as a single unit and forced apart until they found each other again. Pleasure built on pleasure, taking them higher with each thrust, with every breath, until he was poised on the brink of the world. And she was right there with him.

He reared up to watch her passion as he raced with her over the edge. Then he was exploding, splintering, free-falling into the warmth and sanctuary of her waiting embrace.

He didn't want to move. He wanted to stay right here on this crazy single bed with Abby and—he felt her leg slide against his—maybe he could move…if it involved making love with her again. Or they could continue on his comfortable king-size bed.

He levered himself up on one elbow and stroked a finger down her nose, then followed up with a light kiss. 'My bed's bigger.'

She blinked up at him and what he saw in her eyes chilled him to the core. 'I told you. I'm not sleeping in your bed.'

He touched her cheek. So soft, as delicate as an angel's in the moonlight. 'We don't have to sleep.'

'I'm not coming with you.'

Slowly he sat up, propped his arms on his bent knees and looked straight ahead at the wardrobe. Right now it was preferable to looking at Abby and seeing her denial. 'I thought we just shared something incredible. What *was* it to you, then?'

Silence hung thick in the evening air. 'It was good, Zak,' she said at last. There was a waver in her voice. 'The best. But I'm not changing my mind.'

Oh, yes, you will, he said silently as he slid off the bed, and hoped to God he was right.

* * *

For once, Abby didn't look forward to opening Good Vibrations. Facing the clean-up in the shop on too little sleep for one. When she arrived the first things she saw were Zak's shirt and shoes still on the stool where he'd left them. His cologne hung in the air.

She turned the air-conditioner onto High Fan and fully spritzed the area with a room freshener she'd made with a blend of lemon, juniper and peppermint essences.

She didn't see Zak all day.

He turned up as she was shutting the shop at the end of the day. 'Hi. How was your day?'

'Great. Tiring, but that's what I want—lots of clients. How about yours?'

'I've missed you.'

She looked at those blue eyes and yearned with all her heart. 'Zak, don't do this.'

'I'll keep doing this. Until I know it's over.' He closed the space between them until he was within touching distance. 'But it's not over, is it? Not after last night.'

'Zak…'

'Didn't you once tell me I was a stubborn Taurean?' He was standing too close, smelling too enticing… New aftershave? He was also wearing a shirt she hadn't seen before.

'I'm renovating my wardrobe,' he said when he caught her looking. 'What do you think?'

Blue-grey stripe with a maroon silk tie. Different. 'It suits you.'

'Ah. Tomorrow…' his voice switched to business '…we have an important guest visiting Capricorn. I'd like you to schedule two hours free from noon if you would, for an official meet and greet.'

She perked up at the news. 'Who is it?'

'Someone who's looking to retire up here. They seemed

very interested in your Good Vibrations. Maybe they can offer something we may have overlooked. It's good for business. You'll meet them tomorrow. Oh, and dress for a business luncheon.'

'Okay.' She paused. 'About dinner, I'm not—'

'I won't be home till late tonight. I want to make sure everything's right for tomorrow.'

'See you at noon, then.'

Because she couldn't settle that evening, she strolled through the weekly night market along the beachside boardwalk at the top of Cavill Street. A mishmash of colour and light and movement, the sound and smell of the ocean. Holiday-makers and locals alike sauntered past the stalls, eating ice creams and hamburgers.

Not long ago she'd been a visitor. Now she felt like a local. And she was in love with a local, damn his Taurean hide.

She could take Good Vibrations down the coast and start again, without Zak in her life. But she didn't have the money and right now she simply didn't have the energy. It would mean leaving Aurora alone longer than ever.

So she had to find her own apartment, keep her business in Surfers and learn to work alongside Zak. It also meant shutting off her heart.

'Hi.'

Abby felt the familiar adrenaline rush as she looked up from her account book at ten minutes to noon and saw Zak poking his head around the door. And looking good enough to eat in another new shirt and tie.

'Hi. You're not supposed to be here for ten minutes.' She was glad she'd already changed into her business suit. Dragging her hungry gaze away, she shook her head and frowned back at the columns of numbers in front of her. 'I can't get these figures to add up. I'm just not the accountant type.'

Wrong thing to say. Wrong, wrong, wrong, because he came in and stood right behind her. She could feel his body heat burning into her neck. His aftershave teasing her sinuses. Then he leaned down and placed his palms flat on the desk on either side of hers. His breath tickled her ear as he said, 'I'll send Tina down for a couple of hours later.'

She wanted to turn around and kiss that mouth senseless. 'That'd be great. Thanks.'

'So, let's see.' A hairy forearm brushed hers as he reached for her appointment book. 'You've got a good two-hour break.'

His head was so close to hers she swore she could hear him thinking. Then he angled towards her and his eyes fused with hers and she *knew* she'd heard him thinking.

Yeah, what they could have done with a good two hours.

She pushed up and away. 'I'll get my purse. Is your guest here yet?'

'They're running a little behind schedule.' He ushered her down the corridor and into the car park. 'There's something I need to take care of first, and I need you with me.' He opened the passenger door before rounding the hood and buckling up beside her.

'What's going on?'

'Wait and see.' Zak's expression gave nothing away but when she glanced at him Abby saw a slight tension in his jaw and his hands on the steering wheel.

A moment later as they neared Capricorn house Abby frowned, suspicious. 'Why are we going home?'

'Just for a moment…' he said, and turned into the driveway.

And what she saw had her heart rate soaring.

Splashes of potted sunflowers lined the front fence and edged the driveway as he pulled in and came to a stop at the back of the house. Bright yellow ribbons were twined around the veranda posts, their ends fluttering in the breeze.

'Zak. What is all this?' But she thought she knew and…she was afraid to know. Afraid to be right. Afraid to be wrong.

'Abby, look at me.' Infinitely soft words.

Words that scrambled her pulse and turned her legs to jelly. *Think blue*. He tilted her face up with a finger beneath her chin. She was trying to hold the pieces of her heart together but they were slipping away. *Ice-blue. Sky-blue. Lake-blue.* Like his eyes.

Eyes that pierced right through her and saw too much.

'Don't say no to me.' His gaze darkened and never wavered. 'I want you to step out of the car when I open the door and come with me.'

Her mouth must have opened because he pressed a finger to her lips. 'Don't. Say. No.'

She nodded, her nose prickling while she waited for him to come round and open the door. When he did, he placed a simple bouquet of yellow daisies in her arms. She'd never seen anything so beautiful. 'Oh…Zak…'

'Come on, there's more.'

'You've thought of everything,' Abby murmured as they made their way to the veranda.

He yanked his tie so that it hung loose around his neck. 'I hope so, Abby. I damn well hope so.'

She climbed the steps, placed the flowers gently on the table, then walked to the far end to give herself some space. And wait. Zak remained on the top step with his hands in his pockets. The air smelled of flowers and cut grass. Over the fence somewhere she could hear jazz music. She glanced back along the veranda. 'You've bought another rocking chair.'

'One for each of us.'

Her heart stopped, then restarted at double time. Her gaze cut to his. Then it was impossible for her to look away even though his image blurred with unshed moisture. 'You're too busy to sit on a rocking chair for more than two minutes.'

'That's going to change.'

His words stripped her heart bare. But she shook her head. 'I won't leave Aurora alone.'

He nodded. 'We'll get her a rocking chair, too, if you want. She's your family. I'm used to family. When we were kids our great-grandma lived with us till she passed away. There were always relatives staying over. I miss it.

'I miss you. I miss you crowding my space, I miss your laugh, I miss you in my bed.' He was coming towards her with the breeze in his hair and his heart in his eyes. He didn't try to hide his emotion. It was there, in the rigidity of his jaw, the thin line of his lips, the hoarseness of his voice. 'I want to grow old with you, Abby. I want us to sit in those rockers and hold hands when we're ninety and watch our grandchildren play.'

To stop her hands trembling, she curled them into fists and pressed them to her waist. 'You say you miss me. You say you want me in your life. But I have to keep myself safe.' She rushed on. 'I've lived without love for most of my life. I can't…'

'Abby. Baby.' He reached her, took her fists and enclosed them in the rock-solid warmth of his grasp. 'I was getting to that part.' His dimple came out of extended hibernation as he pried her locked fingers apart and entwined them with his. 'As usual, you're one step ahead of me.' He lifted their joined hands to her lips, cutting the rest of her words off. 'Just let me try and get the words out right.'

She waited with her heart beating its way out of her chest as he stepped back and looked into her eyes, and she felt their intensity clear to her soul.

'I love you, Abigail Seymour. When I saw you in the sea that morning I went a little crazy. A lot crazy. I realised I was living in the past, a half-life at best. That the guilt I felt over the circumstances of Diane's death was nothing to what I feel for you. That losing someone you love, losing *you*, is worse than dying.'

Emotion pounded in her heart like the surf she could hear in the distance. It rolled through her veins, crashed in her ears. He loved her? She replayed his words to make sure she'd got it right. *He loved her.*

'I couldn't deal with it,' he continued. 'I had to get away and knock some sanity into myself before I saw you again. I'm sorry it took so damn long. I knew you were hurting. It killed me to see that pain in your eyes, when I left you there on the island, baby. You don't know how I ached to sweep you up and take you back in the chopper with me.' He stroked her cheek with the knuckles of one fist, strength tempered with gentleness. 'But I couldn't. I needed to be whole again.

'You did that for me. You took the pieces and put me back together. You made me look inside myself when I didn't want to see, confronted me at every turn. And you told *me* I was stubborn!' The corners of his mouth curved into a brief smile, then sobered again.

'I don't just want you in my life, Abby. That's not enough. I want to *make* a life with you, to share my life. With you. I made mistakes with Diane. I didn't always put her before work. But you will *always* come first, that I promise you. We can build Capricorn together. Heaven knows, I don't deserve it. I don't deserve you after what I've put you through, but I want a second chance. I'll beg for a second chance if I have to.' He clutched her hands to his chest so she could feel his heart beating a mile a minute beneath. 'Will you marry me, Abby? Will you be the mother of my babies and spend the rest of your life with me?'

'Oh…oh…' She blinked, giving him her wordless answer through blurred eyes, happiness seeping through her body. 'That's perfect. Absolutely perfect.'

'So…' He raised their hands, pressed a kiss to her knuckles. 'What do you say?'

'Kiss me, already.'

'With pleasure.'

And his kiss was filled with all the love she'd seen in his eyes. Warming her lips, filling her heart. Finally, breathless, he drew back. 'Do you have an answer for me?'

She sniffed, smiling through her tears, and reached out to creep her fingers over his chest. 'Do you really need one?'

'I do. I want to hear the words. One word, to be precise.'

'Then the answer's yes. In triplicate. I love you, Zak. I've loved you for so long.' She sniffed. 'No tissue.'

He grinned. 'Go ahead and use my tie.'

'But we have an important luncheon appointment.'

'And I have a stack of new ties.'

A short time later, he ushered her past the poolside café with a light touch at her back. 'We're eating at the Capricorn Bistro.'

'Ooh, flashy,' she murmured, wondering if she was walking on air. She was still reeling with the events of the past half-hour.

'Important,' he told her.

She straightened her lapels again. Tucked a stray hair behind her ear. 'Do I look all right? You still haven't told me what to expect.'

'You look perfect. Wait and see.'

They were met and greeted at the restaurant's reservation desk like— Well, to the wait staff, Zak *was* royalty, she supposed.

Light from the central chandelier glinted off crystal and silver. Tables looked inviting in maroon cloths with snowy-white napkins. Something violin and classical played in the background. Abby's feet sank into the plush cream carpet as they made their way towards the view of the ocean.

An elderly woman with vivid pink hair in flowing tangerine pants and lime-green top was already studying the menu at the table by the window. Her back was towards them but only one woman Abby knew dressed that way…

She slowed, then stopped, surprise and anticipation beating a fast rhythm through her veins. 'Rory?'

The woman turned, her lined face creasing into a smile, and Abby's breath caught, released, caught again. 'It *is* you.' Happiness burst like bubbles as she rushed towards Rory's open arms and held on tight. 'Oh, Rory, it's so, so good to see you.'

'You, too, Abby dearest.' Rory's words were muffled against Abby's cheek.

Still clutching Aurora's hands Abby leaned back. 'You're looking so much better than the last time I saw you! Where's Maddie? When did you get in? Why didn't you let me pick you up at the airport?'

'Your young man picked me up yesterday.'

'My…oh…' Her gaze switched between the two of

them. 'Zak arranged all this?' She felt perilously close to tears again.

'We spent a very pleasant evening getting properly acquainted. He put me up in a luxury suite with twenty-four-hour room service and my own maid on call.' Her face puckered as she smiled up at him. 'I let Maddie go. I don't need a carer with you and—'

'I didn't know you were coming!' Abby almost wailed. 'You never said a word.'

'Zak swore me to secrecy. We've had a couple of long talks by phone.'

'Long talks…' Aurora and Zak had been having long talks and not telling her? If she wasn't so happy she'd have felt left out. 'And did he let you chart his horoscope?' She heard the tinge of sarcasm in her voice.

Aurora squeezed Abby's hand, her smile widening, her eyes twinkling up at him. 'Yes, as a matter of fact he did.'

He hadn't let *Abby* chart his horoscope. No, not quite true. She'd never asked him because she *knew* he thought it was a crock. Her nose prickled ominously. Oh, she was going to tear up again. *Think blue, think blue.*

He'd brought Aurora here to surprise Abby. He knew what she wanted, what she needed. Knew her better than anyone else. 'I need another tissue,' she muttered, fumbling in her pocket. 'Never have a darn tissue when I need one.'

'Come here, baby.' Zak wrapped his arms around her, drew her against his warm masculine body and just held her. 'Use my tie again,' he whispered against her ear. 'The shirt, too, if you need it.'

A wet, sobbing laugh bubbled up as she clutched fistfuls of the crisp new fabric. Dabbed at her eyes with the soft silk tie. Sniffing, she flapped a hand behind her for Aurora.

'Join the party.' And gathered them into a three-way clinch. 'Sorry. Emotional overload.'

Aurora was the first to break away. 'Well, you two can stand there and canoodle all you want, but I'm going to sit right down here and wait for this calorie-laden meal Zak's ordered. The man's positively wicked.'

Oh, yes. Abby knew. Wicked, and tempting and… She hiccupped… Hers. 'Oh, Rory. That man you're accusing of wickedness is my fiancé.'

It was Rory's turn to look wicked as she sat down. 'I know, dear. He's the Taurean I saw in your horoscope.'

Somehow Abby managed to make it through the meal, though she couldn't remember what she'd eaten, or if she'd eaten anything at all. Aurora and Zak talked like old friends. It warmed Abby's heart to see her more animated, more cheery than she'd been in a long time. And Zak, well…for the first time in her experience, he looked alive.

When the two hours were up, and Abby reluctantly excused herself to get back to work, Zak informed her he'd employed another massage therapist for the rest of the day.

Then Zak drove them back home. He walked Aurora inside, outlining his plans for the house, Abby following more slowly.

She passed Zak's bedroom door. And didn't realise she'd stopped moving. Stopped breathing. There was Abby's photo—on his nightstand in her green cocktail dress. The one he'd taken off her that first night they'd made love.

Aurora and Zak were admiring the tropical garden through the back door, but they turned when Abby reached the kitchen. 'Ah, there you are,' Aurora said, and tapped her cane lightly on the floor. 'I'm going to take a nap.'

Zak straightened away from the door frame, walked to the table and unrolled a long sheet of paper. 'If you wouldn't mind, Aurora, before you do, Abby hasn't seen the renovation plans for the studio yet and I'd like to show both of you while you're here.'

Abby looked up in surprise. 'I thought you were turning it into a gym?'

His eyes met hers. 'My plans changed.'

The studio was now officially going to be turned into a bedsit with its own tiny kitchenette and it didn't seem as if anything had been overlooked.

'I'm employing the instant kitchen renovations crew. No more additional working hours.' He pulled Abby to him. 'I've got better things to do with my time.' His eyes were laser-bright and full of promises. 'And Aurora can stay whenever she likes, as long as she likes. Permanently, if she wishes.'

'And until then, Rory, you can sleep in my room.' Abby looked up at the man she loved, who loved her back. 'I've officially moved out.'

It was another half hour before Zak could finally seduce his fiancée into bed to celebrate in private. They decided to keep it secret a few days until they had a ring to show off. Aurora was the only one privy to the happy news. But then she already knew—she'd charted both their horoscopes weeks ago.

Zak played with the ends of Abby's hair as she kissed her way over his chest in the languid aftermath of lovemaking. He couldn't get enough of her hair.

'I want a garden wedding,' she said, between kisses. 'Here, at Capricorn.'

'You can have whatever you want, as long as it's soon.'

She looked up at him and a smile spread over her face. 'Whatever I want, really?' She settled in beside him. 'The truth, then. When was the first time you knew you loved me?'

'Easy. The first night I came home and you'd left the porch light on for me. I realised I'd been marking time, that my life had been on hold, not for the reasons I'd clung to but because I'd been waiting for you. Of course, I didn't know it at the time.'

'I'll always wait for you, Zak.' And her kiss warmed him all the way to his toes.

'No more waiting. You won't need to leave the light on again,' he murmured against her mouth, absorbing the sweet taste of her love. 'We'll drive home together from this day forward.'

Smiling, Abby rose up on one elbow to look at him. His eyes, warm with wanting and full of love, smiled back at her.

He was home, he was whole, and, best of all, he was hers. She sighed with satisfaction and kissed him again.

Mission accomplished.

* * * * *

Here's a sneak peek at
THE CEO'S CHRISTMAS PROPOSITION,
the first in USA TODAY *bestselling author*
Merline Lovelace's HOLIDAYS ABROAD *trilogy*
coming in November 2008.

American Devon McShay is about to get the Christmas
surprise of a lifetime when she meets her new client,
sexy billionaire Caleb Logan, for the very first time.

Silhouette®
Desire

Available November 2008

Her breath whistled out in a sigh of relief when he exited Customs. Devon recognized him right away from the newspaper and magazine articles her friend and partner Sabrina had looked up during her frantic prep work.

Caleb John Logan, Jr. Thirty-one. Six-two. With jet-black hair, laser-blue eyes and a linebacker's shoulders under his charcoal-gray cashmere overcoat. His jaw-dropping good looks didn't score him any points with Devon. She'd learned the hard way not to trust handsome heartbreakers like Cal Logan.

But he was a client. An important one. And she was willing to give someone who'd served a hitch in the marines before earning a B.S. from the University of Oregon, an MBA from Stanford and his first million at the ripe old age of twenty-six the benefit of the doubt.

Right up until he spotted the hot-pink pashmina, that is.

Devon knew the flash of color was more visible than the sign she held up with his name on it. So she wasn't surprised when Logan picked her out of the crowd and cut in her direction. She'd just plastered on her best businesswoman smile when he whipped an arm around her waist. The next moment she was sprawled against his cashmere-covered chest.

"Hello, brown eyes."

Swooping down, he covered her mouth with his.

Sheer astonishment kept Devon rooted to the spot for a few seconds while her mind whirled chaotically. Her first thought was that her client had downed a few too many drinks during the long flight. Her second, that he'd mistaken the kind of escort and consulting services her company provided. Her third shoved everything else out of her head.

The man could kiss!

His mouth moved over hers with a skill that ignited sparks at a half dozen flash points throughout her body. Devon hadn't experienced that kind of spontaneous combustion in a while. A *long* while.

The sparks were still popping when she pushed off his chest, only now they fueled a flush of anger.

"Do you always greet women you don't know with a lip-lock, Mr. Logan?"

A smile crinkled the skin at the corners of his eyes. "As a matter of fact, I don't. That was from Don."

"Huh?"

"He said he owed you one from New Year's Eve two years ago and made me promise to deliver it."

She stared up at him in total incomprehension. Logan hooked a brow and attempted to prompt a nonexistent memory.

"He abandoned you at the Waldorf. Five minutes before midnight. To deliver twins."

"I don't have a clue who or what you're…"

Understanding burst like a water balloon.

"Wait a sec. Are you talking about Sabrina's old boyfriend? Your buddy, who's now an ob-gyn doc?"

It was Logan's turn to look startled. He recovered faster than Devon had, though. His smile widened into a rueful grin.

"I take it you're not Sabrina Russo."

"No, Mr. Logan, I am *not*."

* * * * *

Be sure to look for
THE CEO'S CHRISTMAS PROPOSITION
by Merline Lovelace.
Available in November 2008 wherever books are sold,
including most bookstores, supermarkets, drugstores
and discount stores.

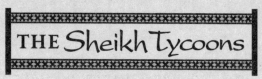

Exclusively His

Back in his bed—and he's better than ever!

Whether you shared his bed for one night—
or five years—certain men are impossible to forget!
He might be your ex, but when you're back in his bed,
the passion is not just hot, it's scorching!

Things get tricky for sensible Veronica when
she unexpectedly meets Lucien again after one
night in Paris. And now he's determined to
seduce her back into his bed....

PUBLIC SCANDAL, PRIVATE MISTRESS
by Susan Napier

#2777

Available in November.

*Look out for more Exclusively His novels
in Harlequin Presents in 2009!*

I ♥ HARLEQUIN® Presents

BROUGHT TO YOU BY FANS OF HARLEQUIN PRESENTS.

We are its editors and authors
and biggest fans—and we'd
love to hear from YOU!

**Subscribe today to our online blog at
www.iheartpresents.com**

REQUEST YOUR FREE BOOKS!

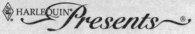 **HARLEQUIN®** *Presents* ®

2 FREE NOVELS
PLUS 2
FREE GIFTS!

PASSION
GUARANTEED
SEDUCTION

YES! Please send me 2 FREE Harlequin Presents® novels and my 2 FREE gifts (gifts are worth about $10). After receiving them, if I don't wish to receive any more books, I can return the shipping statement marked "cancel". If I don't cancel, I will receive 6 brand-new novels every month and be billed just $4.05 per book in the U.S. or $4.74 per book in Canada, plus 25¢ shipping and handling per book and applicable taxes, if any*. That's a savings of close to 15% off the cover price! I understand that accepting the 2 free books and gifts places me under no obligation to buy anything. I can always return a shipment and cancel at any time. Even if I never buy another book, the two free books and gifts are mine to keep forever.

106 HDN ERRW 306 HDN ERRL

Name	(PLEASE PRINT)	
Address		Apt. #
City	State/Prov.	Zip/Postal Code

Signature (if under 18, a parent or guardian must sign)

Mail to the **Harlequin Reader Service:**
IN U.S.A.: P.O. Box 1867, Buffalo, NY 14240-1867
IN CANADA: P.O. Box 609, Fort Erie, Ontario L2A 5X3

Not valid to current subscribers of Harlequin Presents books.

Want to try two free books from another line?
Call 1-800-873-8635 or visit www.morefreebooks.com.

* Terms and prices subject to change without notice. N.Y. residents add applicable sales tax. Canadian residents will be charged applicable provincial taxes and GST. Offer not valid in Quebec. This offer is limited to one order per household. All orders subject to approval. Credit or debit balances in a customer's account(s) may be offset by any other outstanding balance owed by or to the customer. Please allow 4 to 6 weeks for delivery. Offer available while quantities last.

Your Privacy: Harlequin Books is committed to protecting your privacy. Our Privacy Policy is available online at www.eHarlequin.com or upon request from the Reader Service. From time to time we make our lists of customers available to reputable third parties who may have a product or service of interest to you. If you would prefer we not share your name and address, please check here. ☐

HP08R

MARRIED BY CHRISTMAS

For better or worse—she'll be his by Christmas!

As the festive season approaches, these darkly handsome Mediterranean men are looking forward to unwrapping their brand-new brides.... Whether they're living luxuriously in London or flying by private jet to their glamorous European villas, these arrogant, commanding tycoons need a wife...and they'll have one— by Christmas!

HIRED: THE ITALIAN'S CONVENIENT MISTRESS
by CAROL MARINELLI (Book #29)

THE SPANISH BILLIONAIRE'S CHRISTMAS BRIDE
by MAGGIE COX (Book #30)

CLAIMED FOR THE ITALIAN'S REVENGE
by NATALIE RIVERS (Book #31)

THE PRINCE'S ARRANGED BRIDE
by SUSAN STEPHENS (Book #32)

Happy holidays from Harlequin Presents!

Available in November.

HARLEQUIN *Presents*

Coming Next Month

#2771 RUTHLESSLY BEDDED BY THE ITALIAN BILLIONAIRE
Emma Darcy
Ruthless

#2772 RAFAEL'S SUITABLE BRIDE Cathy Williams
Italian Husbands

#2773 MENDEZ'S MISTRESS Anne Mather
Latin Lovers

#2774 THE SHEIKH'S WAYWARD WIFE Sandra Marton
The Sheikh Tycoons

#2775 BEDDED BY THE GREEK BILLIONAIRE Kate Walker
Greek Tycoons

#2776 THE MEDITERRANEAN PRINCE'S CAPTIVE VIRGIN
Robyn Donald
The Mediterranean Princes

#2777 PUBLIC SCANDAL, PRIVATE MISTRESS Susan Napier
Exclusively His

#2778 A NIGHT WITH THE SOCIETY PLAYBOY Ally Blake
Nights of Passion

Plus, look out for the fabulous new collection *Married by Christmas* in Harlequin Presents® EXTRA:

#29 HIRED: THE ITALIAN'S CONVENIENT MISTRESS
Carol Marinelli

#30 THE SPANISH BILLIONAIRE'S CHRISTMAS BRIDE
Maggie Cox

#31 CLAIMED FOR THE ITALIAN'S REVENGE
Natalie Rivers

#32 THE PRINCE'S ARRANGED BRIDE
Susan Stephens

HPCNM1008